THE GUNSMITH

439

Blackbeard's Gun

Books by J.R. Roberts
(Robert J. Randisi)

The Gunsmith series

The Lady Gunsmith series

Angel Eyes series

Tracker series

Mountain Jack Pike series

COMING SOON!

The Gunsmith
440 – Lost Man

For more information visit:
www.speakingvolumes.us

THE GUNSMITH

439

Blackbeard's Gun

J.R. Roberts

SPEAKING VOLUMES, LLC
NAPLES, FLORIDA
2018

Blackbeard's Gun

ISBN 978-1-62815-865-6

Prologue

Ocracoke Inlet, N.C.
1717

Captain Edward Teach, known far and wide to all as Blackbeard the Pirate, stared out at the water of Ocracoke Inlet. His balcony was a perfect place for him to spot incoming ships. The Governor of Pennsylvania had put out a warrant for his arrest but as of the end of August, he had returned to his pirating ways, mostly in the Delaware Bay. He doubted they'd find him here, but kept watch, nonetheless.

Teach was a tall man with broad shoulders. The *sobriquet* "Blackbeard" had been well earned by his long, flowing black facial hair, which he took to winding ribbons throughout.

"Edward?"

He turned and looked at his "wife," the daughter of a local farmer. Of course, they weren't married, but he had convinced her that the impromptu wedding was real, and that Crawly, one of his crewmen, was a licensed parson.

The point had been to get her into bed, and that was what he had done—all night. Now she stood in the French doorway, totally naked, beckoning to him. At 20, she was a tall, full-bodied girl, strong as an ox.

Teach was in his 37th year and thought that trying to keep up with the girl all night had brought him near to a heart attack. For a virgin, she had taken to the sex readily, eagerly even, and he was surprised at how insatiable she was. Sometimes, he thought, you do have to be careful what you wish for.

"Captain!"

The voice came from beneath them. Teach looked over the edge of the balcony. The naked girl came and stood next to him.

"Mr. Franklin," Teach said. "What is it?"

"The gunmaker is here, sir," the crewman said. "With your new weapons."

"Take him to the sitting room," Teach said. "I will dress and be right down."

"Aye, sir."

He turned to look at the naked girl.

"You better hurry on home, my dear."

"But I am home, Edward," she said. "We are married, remember? My place is with my husband."

Teach stared at her, trying to remember her name.

"Well, stay here, then, love," he said. "I have to go down and see my pistolmaker. I shan't be long."

"Hurry back, dear Edward," she said, looking at him with love in her eyes.

Teach dressed quickly, donning his dark trousers and blue silk shirt then pulling on his knee-high boots. He thought about his velvet coat, but it wasn't necessary for this occasion. He hurried downstairs, where he found Crawly waiting.

"He's in the sittin' room, Captain," the man said.

"All right, Crawly. I'll see to him; you go upstairs and tell that girl to go home."

"But Captain, she thinks the two of you are married."

"Thanks to you, Crawly," Teach said. "So when she sees you, she'll know we're not. And that's when you hustle her off home to her father."

"But . . . if she tells her father, then we'll have to kill 'im."

Blackbeard slapped Crawly on the shoulder and said, "I'll leave the details to you, lad," and hurried off to the sitting room to meet his pistolmaker.

***

As Teach entered the room the pistolmaker spread all the weapons out on a cloth, across the long, oak table.

"Captain!" the man exclaimed, waving his hand. "Here they are, just as you described."

Teach approached the table to examine the weapons. At the same time he could hear the girl screaming as

3

Crawly gave her the sad news, and tried to hustle her out of the house.

"The flintlock," the pistolmaker said, touching the weapon with his forefinger, "the blunderbuss—"

"Quiet!" Teach snapped.

"Yes, Captain!"

Teach picked up the blunderbuss, built to his personal specifications. This gun would fire anything he chose to fill the barrel with and, at close range, would tear a man to shreds. When Teach and his men took a ship, and boarded it, the engagements were in close quarters.

He put the blunderbuss down and picked up the flintlock. Again, the man had built to his specifications. It was double-barreled, with a hammer and trigger on each side. After firing the blunderbuss he would toss it down and take one of these from his belt.

"How many?" he asked.

"Six, sir," the pistolmaker said. "six flintlocks, just as you requested."

"Excellent."

He set one down, picked up another, and then a third.

"Of course, we will have to test them," he said.

"Of course, sir. We can go outside and do it right now."

Teach could still hear the girl screaming. If Crawly didn't get rid of her soon, he knew who he would be testing these weapons on.

And then there was silence.

Lucky girl.

"Very well, my good man," he said, waving with a flourish, "it's outside we go!"

Chapter One

Clint Adams read the telegram while sitting in Rick's Place, in Labyrinth, Texas.

"Must be interesting," Rick said.

"Hmm?"

"You've read it three times."

Clint looked at Rick, seated across the table from him, and then picked up his coffee and pushed his empty breakfast plate away.

"Do you know what a blunderbuss is?" Clint asked.

Rick frowned.

"It's some kind of gun, isn't it? Eighteenth century?"

"Maybe even seventeenth," Clint said.

"That's about all I know," Rick admitted. "Is there more?"

"Well," Clint said, "it was an early version of a shot-gun."

"Now that I didn't know. What kind of shells?"

"None," Clint said. "It would fire anything you stuffed into the barrel—usually something metal, like nails."

"Ouch. So what's in the telegram?"

"It's from somebody in North Carolina," Clint said. "They're asking me to come and authenticate a gun."

"A blunderbuss?"

Clint nodded.

"Why you? I mean, I know you're an authority on guns, but can't they find somebody closer?"

Clint shrugged.

"I don't know. Maybe everybody else turned them down."

"North Carolina," Rick said. "You ever been there?"

"Once," Clint said, "during the war. Pinkerton sent me down there."

"What for?"

"Undercover work," Clint said. "I was young and looked younger, so he put me in a Confederate stable. I cleaned stalls for three mounts, while keeping my ears open."

"And not since then?"

"Nope."

"Any hankerin' to go back?"

"Not really."

"Then send back a telegram that says 'no,'" Rick recommended.

"Not so fast," Clint said. "I may not have an urge to go back to North Carolina to revisit my youth, but this blunderbuss business."

"Have you ever seen one?"

"Several times," Clint said, "at gun shows and in museums."

"So what would entice you to travel from here to North Carolina?" Rick asked.

"This one," Clint said, "is supposed to have belonged to Edward Teach."

"Who?"

"Blackbeard the Pirate."

***

Usually, when Clint returned to Labyrinth for some rest and relaxation, Rick would have a new saloon girl working for him, and Clint would get to know her. Then, when he came back months later, she would be gone and there would be a new one to take her place. This time, however, Clint had only arrived two days ago, and already the telegram was trying to lure him away. He had not had time to make the acquaintance of any of Rick's new girls.

There was nothing to keep him in Labyrinth, except that he wanted to give some time off to Eclipse. The Darley Arabian was no spring chicken, anymore, and riding all over the country tended to take it out of him. Clint was even considering a new horse, but that could wait. If he decided to go to North Carolina, he could make the entire trip by rail.

"You sure you want to do this?" Rick asked. "That's a long time to spend on trains."

"Longer in the saddle."

"But you like riding," Rick said. "And you can make stops along the way."

Clint waved the telegram and said, "There seems to be some urgency. They've offered to wire me the money for travel, as well as a down payment on my fee."

Rick laughed.

"You don't need either one."

"No, I don't," Clint said, "but how can I pass up the chance to see, to hold in my hand, Blackbeard the Pirate's blunderbuss."

"So you just got here, and off you go, again."

"So it seems."

"And what about Eclipse?"

"He can stay," Clint said. "I know you'll look after him for me."

"Count on it," Rick said.

"Then I'll leave town tomorrow," Clint said. "Stagecoach to Fort Worth, and then the rest of the way by rail."

"I never knew you to be so interested in pirates, Clint," Rick said.

"Maybe," Clint said, "where there's a pirate gun, there might also be a pirate lady."

He stood up.

"So what're you going to do with the rest of the day?" Rick asked.

"I've got some telegrams to send."

Chapter Two

When Clint disembarked from the train in Ocracoke, North Carolina, there was a man waiting for him at the station.

"Mr. Adams?"

Clint was wearing his gun and carrying a carpetbag. He put the bag down to shake hands with the tall, young-ish, bespectacled man.

"That's right," Clint said.

"My name is Calendar," the man said, "Ted Calendar. I have a buggy waiting outside."

"Great," Clint started to bend to pick up his bag.

"Let me get that," Calendar said, grabbing it quickly. "This way."

Clint followed the young man through the busy train station to the street outside, where a single-horse buggy was waiting, with a driver.

"Here we go," Calendar said.

The driver dropped down to grab the bag and stowed it in the rear of the buggy, while Clint and Calendar climbed into the passenger seat. As the driver climbed up and grabbed the reins, Clint leaned forward and grabbed the driver's arm.

"Hold on a minute," he said.

"Yessir."

"Is something wrong?" the young man asked.

"Yes," Clint said, "I don't know who you are."

"Well," he said, "I told you my name is—"

"Yes, you told me your name," Clint said, cutting him off, "but that doesn't tell me who you are. I was sent a telegram by a Mister Walter Fairchild."

"Oh, yes," Calendar said, "I work for Mr. Fairchild."

"Doing what?"

"I'm his assistant. I do things like—well, this, picking up guests at the train station."

"And taking me where?"

"To one of our finest hotels."

Abruptly, Clint stood up and stepped out of the buggy.

"Uh, but—"

"Can you give me my bag, please?" Clint called up the driver.

"Yessir."

He jumped back down, collected Clint's bag from the rear of the buggy, and handed it to him.

"Thanks," Clint said. "I won't be needing you." He looked at Calendar. "Or you."

"I don't understand."

"You weren't sent here by Mr. Fairchild."

The young man frowned.

"What makes you say that?"

"Because I exchanged telegrams with Mr. Fairchild," Clint said, "and he invited me to stay at his home. Not in a hotel."

"Well, yes, but—"

"You'd better move on, sonny," Clint said. "I don't know who sent you, but Fairchild also told me there are others interested in these pieces."

"Mr. Adams—"

"Get!"

The buggy had already left, so young Mr. Calendar began walking away . . . quickly.

Clint turned and walked back to the train station's front entrance. A woman was standing there with her arms folded, studying him.

"Clint Adams?" she asked.

"That's right."

"I thought so at first," she said, "then I saw you walking away with that young man." She put her hand out. "Charlotte Goodrich. I work for Mr. Fairchild."

"Is that so?" He shook her hand. "He send you to pick me up?"

"Yes, he did," she said. "He wants me to take you to his house."

Clint studied her for a moment. She was dressed for business in a severe suit that did little to hide her femininity. Seemed to be in her 30's, with brown hair cut short.

"Okay, then," Clint said. "Lead the way."

"I've got a buggy around the corner," she said.

Clint followed the lady to the side of the train station, where there was another one-horse buggy, like the first one.

"Toss your bag in the back," she said.

"Where's the driver?" he asked, after obeying.

She grinned.

"That would be me. Hop in the back."

Now this made more sense, so he did like she said and got in the hooded back. She climbed up into the driver's seat, picked up the reins and snapped them at the horse.

"Is it a long ride?" he called out to her.

"Not at all," she said, looking over her shoulder. "Just sit back, relax and enjoy the countryside."

Clint figured he would try to do that, but without much success. The short time he had spent in North Carolina during the war had not been pleasant.

He thought he'd never go back there.

Chapter Three

The house was a huge Southern-style mansion, with four white pillars in front. Charlotte Goodrich drove him to the front door. As Clint stepped down from the buggy, the door opened, and a large well-dressed man came out.

"Mr. Adams!" he said, from the top of the stairs.

"Mr. Fairchild?"

As the man came down the stairs, he seemed to age. Initially Clint had guessed 50s, but now that he was close he could see the man was in his 60s.

They shook hands and the man looked at Charlotte Goodrich.

"Any trouble finding him, Charlotte?"

"No trouble at all, sir."

"Good, good," he said. "Come inside with us, Charlotte. I'll have someone take care of the buggy. Mr. Adams?"

"Lead the way, sir," Clint said, grabbing his carpetbag.

Fairchild led the way up the stairs and into the house. The entry hall had marble floor tiles, and their footsteps made quite a lot of noise crossing it.

They continued to a stairway, where Fairchild turned and smiled.

"I'll show you to your room, Mr. Adams," he said. "You probably would like to freshen up before we talk."

"That sounds good," Clint said. "Thank you."

"Charlotte, why don't you go to the kitchen and tell cook we'll have an early lunch in the diningroom."

"Yes, sir."

She turned and went off to the kitchen. Fairchild showed Clint upstairs.

"This is your room," he said, stopping in front of an open door. "There's a water closet down the hall. When you're refreshed, you can come down to lunch."

"Thank you, Mr. Fairchild," Clint said.

"Did you have any trouble during your trip?" the man asked.

"Only when I got here," Clint said. "A young man tried to get me into a buggy, said you sent him to take me to a hotel."

"What?" Fairchild said. "I only sent Charlotte to pick you up."

"Yes, I figured that out for myself," Clint said. "Let's talk about it later."

"Of course," Fairchild said. "See you in a few minutes."

"Thank you for your hospitality," Clint said.

"Thank you for coming."

Fairchild went off down the hall and Clint entered the room, put his bag on the bed, which had an incredibly firm mattress.

He sat down, wondered if he should have questioned the young man at the train station a little more. But he had only just gotten off the train and thought that Fairchild would know who the young man was.

He decided to ask more about him when he got downstairs . . .

***

After washing up, Clint went downstairs to the dinngroom and found Fairchild and Charlotte sitting at a long, wooden table.

"Ah, there you are, Mr. Adams," the man said. "Good. Charlotte, would you ask cook to serve?"

"Yes, sir."

"Sit, sir, sit," he said to Clint. "My cook is the best in the county. You won't find anything better in any restaurant."

Charlotte returned, and then the cook—an older, grey-haired woman—came in and served lunch. It looked more like an early dinner. There were pieces of chicken prepared in a way he had never seen or tasted, and vegetables to match.

"Was I wrong?" Fairchild asked, after Clint had a taste or two.

"No, you were quite right," Clint said. "This is delicious. What is it?"

"The cook says she calls it chicken fricassee," Charlotte said.

"It's very tasty," Clint said. "Uh, do you mind if we talk while we eat?"

"Not at all," his host said. "I'm sure you're very curious about the pieces I telegraphed you about."

"And apparently others are interested, too," Clint said. "Any idea who that man trying to snatch me from the train station was?"

"None," Fairchild said.

"Maybe if I describe him a little more," Clint said, and did so, right down to his spectacles.

"I can't put a name to the description, at the moment," Fairchild said, "can you, Charlotte?"

"No, sir."

"He must be working for someone," Clint said. "How many others are interested?"

"There are several parties," Fairchild said. "Some of them are even laying claim to the guns."

"Laying claim?"

"They're claiming to be related to Blackbeard the Pirate," Charlotte explained.

"Are they?" Clint asked. "I mean, could they be?"

"No," Fairchild said. "They can't be. None of them are from England. Blackbeard was from England."

Chapter Four

After the fine lunch Clint gave his compliments to the cook, and followed Fairchild and Charlotte to the library.

"Sherry?" Fairchild offered.

"I'm not really a sherry man," Clint said. "I usually drink beer."

"Well," Fairchild said, "I suppose we could go to a local saloon—"

"No, no," Clint said. "I'm fine. You have your sherry and we'll talk."

"All right."

Fairchild poured a glass for himself and one for Charlotte without asking.

There were three armchairs in the room, so they all sat.

"Where are the guns, now?" Clint asked.

"They're in our museum," Fairchild said, "under lock and key."

"Can anybody get to them?"

"I can take you over there tomorrow to show you the guns, and our set-up," Fairchild said.

"Fine."

"We thought, since you were going to be here anyway, that you might give us some advice about security."

"I can do that," Clint said. "Isn't it early enough for us to go over there now?"

"Actually," Fairchild said, "I can't. I have an appointment in about an hour."

"How about Charlotte?"

Fairchild and Charlotte exchanged a glance.

"I suppose she could take you over there," Fairchild said, "but I'd rather not have you handle the guns until I'm present, too. If that's all right."

"At least I could take a gander at them, today," Clint said. "And your security."

"Okay," Fairchild said. "Charlotte?"

"Yes, sir." She looked at Clint. "We could go any time you wish."

"I'll just go upstairs and get my hat and jacket," Clint said.

"Jacket?" Fairchild asked. "It's rather warm."

"I'm just thinking about this," Clint said, indicating the gun on his hip.

"Can't you leave it behind?" Fairchild asked.

"Not a chance," Clint said. "First time I go out without my gun could be the last time."

"Oh, I'm sorry," Fairchild said. "Because of your reputation, of course. I should have known."

Clint started from the room, then stopped at the door and turned back.

"Mr. Fairchild, can you tell me where you got my name?" Clint asked.

"From a man who claims to be a friend of yours," the man said. "He was in the museum, heard me talking about the Blackbeard pieces, and told me about you."

"And where to send me a telegram?"

"Yes, exactly."

"Got a name?"

"It was Roper," Fairchild said, "Talbot Roper. He said he was a private detective. When I asked him if he could help with security he said he was busy, but that I should contact you about that, too."

"Tal is the best detective in the country, private or otherwise," Clint said.

"All the more reason for me to hire you, then," Fairchild said. "His recommendation was very high, indeed."

Clint looked at Charlotte.

"I'll be right down."

"I'll be out front in the buggy."

As Clint left the room, he was sure he heard Fairchild say something to Charlotte fairly urgently, under his breath so Clint wouldn't hear.

***

As Clint collected his hat and jacket, he wondered just how much underhandedness he was going to be able to put up with just to see and touch Blackbeard's guns?

Already somebody had tried to pull the wool over his eyes, get him away from the man who had contacted him. And he had the feeling Fairchild wasn't telling him everything. Charlotte certainly wasn't. But he did want to hold those guns in his hands before he made any decisions.

When he came downstairs Walter Fairchild was nowhere to be seen but, as promised, Charlotte was waiting out front, in the buggy.

Clint climbed up into the driver's seat with her, instead of the back.

"Do you mind if I ride up here with you?" he asked.

"Not at all, if that's what you want," she said.

Then he snatched the reins from her hands.

"And, why don't you let me drive? You can sit back, give directions . . . and answer some questions."

Chapter Five

"Questions about what?" Charlotte asked, as they got underway.

"Oh, the state of affairs around here," Clint said. "Who's who, what's what, that sort of thing."

"Why do you need to know that?"

"Someone has already tried to keep me away from your boss," Clint said. "I'd like to know who sent him."

"I don't know that," she claimed.

"How long have you lived here?"

"All my life."

"And how long have you worked for Mr. Fairchild?"

"Three years, now."

"Then you know everything that goes on around here," Clint said. "I'm also interested in the museum, and how Fairchild came to be in possession of the guns that may or may not have belonged to Blackbeard."

"I can answer some of those questions," she said, "but not all."

"I'll start with some, then . . ." he said.

***

Walter Fairchild was a wealthy man, but he did not own the museum. He simply sat on the board of directors who ran it.

"The museum has a curator," Charlotte told him, "who you'll be very interested in meeting."

"And why is that?" Clint asked.

"You'll know as soon as I make the introduction."

"So if he doesn't own it, and only sits on the board, why is he the one paying me?"

"Mr. Fairchild wants to make very certain that these guns are genuine, and that the museum's security is impenetrable."

"So he's spending his own money to make sure of all that," Clint said.

"Yes."

"And what's he not telling me?"

"I beg your pardon?"

"As I left the room just now he whispered something to you," Clint told her. "What was it?"

"Mr. Adams," she said, "if Mr. Fairchild has something to tell you that he hasn't told you yet, that's up to him. I work for him, therefore he has my loyalty."

Clint looked at the girl, who seemed to be very much in earnest.

"That's very commendable," he said, as they approached a fork in the road. "Which way?"

***

When they reached the museum, Charlotte had Clint drive the buggy around to the back where there were several others parked. There were, however, none in the front.

"Is it open to the public?" he asked.

"Usually," she said, as he helped her down, "but because of the Blackbeard display, it's been closed."

"Why's Blackbeard so important?" Clint asked.

"He was in this area," she said. "Didn't you know?"

"I thought he was the scourge of the West Indies," Clint said. "At least, that's what I heard."

"He also robbed ships in Delaware Bay, and off the coast of North Carolina," she informed him. She led him to a rear door. "We can go in this way."

"I get it," Clint said. "He'll be a draw here at the museum because he was local."

"Exactly."

They walked up a back staircase and into a vast interior with high ceilings and marble floors.

"I'll take you to meet the curator," Charlotte said.

"First," Clint said, "I'd like to see the guns."

"Very well," Charlotte said, changing direction. "This way, then."

She led him through the museum, past many displays in which he had no interest. Finally, they reached a section that was roped off, and covered by a tarpaulin.

"You'll have to pull back the covering" she told him.

"Of course."

He stepped forward, ducked beneath the ropes and did as she asked.

And there they were.

Two weapons. One was a flintlock, with two barrels, two hammers and two triggers. The other was a blunderbuss with a long barrel that could be filled with so many things, all of which would become deadly once they had been launched.

"What do you think?" she asked.

He turned and looked at her. She had remained behind the ropes.

"It's beautiful workmanship," he said, "but I can't tell much else by just looking at them. Do you have a key to this display?"

"No," she said. "Only the curator does, but she won't open it."

"Why not?"

"Not without a member of the board present," Charlotte went on, "and preferably Mr. Fairchild."

"Okay, then." He took one last look before covering the display again. "Let's go and meet the curator."

Chapter Six

Charlotte led Clint through the museum to a section of offices, to the door marked CURATOR. Charlotte knocked, and while Clint didn't hear anyone call out "Come in," she opened the door.

"Miss Kennedy," she said, "this is Clint Adams, the man Mr. Fairchild brought in to authenticate the Blackbeard guns. Mr. Adams, this is our museum curator, Miss Jayne Kennedy."

Clint saw the woman behind the desk stand up, and was stunned—not by her beauty, but her stature. Oh, she was beautiful, all right, but she looked like an amazon, standing over 6 feet tall as she came around the desk. She had long, shining blonde hair, and the clearest, bluest eyes he had ever seen. No, they weren't blue, they were . . . lavender, like the note paper and blotter she had on her desk. It must have been her favorite color, and he could see why.

"Mr. Adams," she said, in a throaty voice, "I'm very happy to meet you."

"Miss Kennedy," he said, "same here."

They shook hands. She was a solidly built woman with a firm handshake, wearing a business suit much like the one Charlotte was wearing. Both women were obviously very feminine, despite the severe cut of their clothing, but while Miss Kennedy was firmly built, Charlotte was very slender, and stood about 5 foot 4 inches tall. There seemed like a 10 year difference in the women's age, with Jayne Kennedy probably being close to 40.

"Please, sit," she said, going back around the desk and sitting. "Charlotte—"

"I have an errand to run," Charlotte said, cutting her off. "Can I leave him with you?"

"Of course."

Charlotte looked at Clint. "I'll be back for you."

"Fine." It wasn't the worst prospect, being alone with Jayne Kennedy.

Charlotte left, closing the door behind her.

"I've seen the guns—" Clint started.

"What? How?"

"Charlotte showed me the display case."

"She shouldn't have done that," the woman said. "No one is supposed to look at them without a board member present."

"Don't blame her, Miss Kennedy," Clint said. "I pretty much forced her. Besides, I couldn't touch them."

"Oh, I suppose it's all right," she said. "And you might as well call me Jayne, since you'll probably be in and out of here."

"And you can call me Clint," he said. "I understand I can't touch the guns until later, but maybe you can tell me more about them than Charlotte did."

"I'd be happy to," Jayne said. "How much do you know?"

"Just a few facts about your board, Walter Fairchild, and about why these guns are so important to this museum."

"Blackbeard the Pirate is a legendary local figure," she replied. "That's the simple reason why these pieces are important to the museum."

"Where were they found?"

"In a cave on our coast," she said. "Some men were actually out there looking for the remains of some old shipwrecks and found them."

"And nothing else?"

"Nothing of equal value," she told him. "Some remnants, which will revolve around these two pieces, once we get them cleaned up. But they are the jewels of our collection."

"Understandable," Clint said, and then added, "if they're genuine."

"And proving or disproving that is your job," Jayne said.

"Maybe we can talk more about it over supper tonight," Clint said. "I have no idea where to get a good steak."

Jayne almost smiled but managed to hide it.

"I thought you'd be dining with Mr. Fairchild," she said. "Or, perhaps, Charlotte."

"I don't think so," he said. "If you don't accept, I think I'll be eating alone."

"Well," she said, "we can't have that. After all, you're a guest, here."

"Then you accept?"

"I do."

"Good. I'll see you tonight," he said, standing.

"I'll come by Mr. Fairchild's house and pick you up," Jayne said. "I'll be the host, tonight."

"That suits me," Clint said.

"I know just the place to take you for a steak."

"I'm looking forward to it."

He turned and left the office.

***

Clint found Charlotte waiting for him behind the museum, with the buggy.

"So, did she do it?" she asked him.

"Do what?"

"Charm the pants off you?" Charlotte said. "That's what she does."

"You got something against Miss Kennedy, Charlotte?" he asked.

"You mean besides the fact that she's got my job?" Charlotte asked.

"She replaced you as curator?"

"I was supposed to be named curator after working for Fairchild for three years. Instead, she came along and charmed the job right out from under me."

"Well," he said, "I kept my pants on, but she is taking me out for a steak later."

"That figures," she said. "So, where to now?"

"Any chance you could take me where they found the guns?" Clint asked.

"You mean the caves?" she asked. "Not dressed like this."

"But we could get there?"

"Yes, with some walking."

"Can you change into something more . . . appropriate?" he asked.

"I'll have to go home."

"That's okay," he said. "I can wait. It's early, and we've got plenty of light left."

"Get in, then," she said. "It's about half an hour away from here."

"Mind if I sit up top again?"
"No," she said, "but I drive, this time!"

Chapter Seven

Charlotte drove them to a neighborhood of two-story houses, bringing the buggy to a stop in front of one of them.

"You own this?" he asked.

"I wish. I just rent the second floor."

"I see," Clint said. "Well, I'll wait out here while you go change your clothes."

"It won't take long," she promised, and went inside.

***

He waited by the buggy, stroking the horse's neck and thinking about the two women, Charlotte and Jayne. He had seen Charlotte with Fairchild. Initially, his impression was that she respected him, and he trusted her. But now, being told that he gave the job to Jayne over Charlotte, that relationship seemed to be very different.

He looked up at Charlotte's window, wondering what exactly she had meant by "charming the pants off," when talking about Jayne Kennedy?

He heard a door close, turned and saw Charlotte coming back down the walk, wearing what looked like a work shirt and jeans, and a pair of boots.

"Ready?" she asked.

"When you are," he said, and they climbed back aboard.

***

She drove them down to a beach, getting as close as she could.

"The caves are down along the shoreline," she said. "We'll have to walk from here."

"Have you been down here before?" he asked.

"Once, with Mr. Fairchild," she said. "He was complaining the entire time about getting sand in his shoes, but he wanted to see where the pieces had been found."

She put the brake on the buggy, so the horses wouldn't be going anywhere, and led the way down to the beach.

It had been a while since Clint had seen the ocean like this, so he took a moment to stand and watch as the tide went in and out.

"What is that out there?" he asked, pointing.

"That's Ocracoke Island," Charlotte said. "It's said that Blackbeard stayed there. Pretty, isn't it?"

"It is," he said. He looked at her, then, and noticed she looked prettier now that she was out of her work clothes. "Very pretty."

"Come on," she said. "It's a bit of a walk."

He followed her through the sand along the beach, and when they came around a turn he saw the caves.

"I assume when the tide comes in they flood?" he asked.

"Exactly," she said. "Fairchild figures the tide might have brought the pieces in, or they could have been buried there, and the tide unearthed them.

"They both sound right."

Now they were walking between the water and the rocks.

"It's here," she said.

"I don't see it."

"You wouldn't," she said. "It was found completely by accident. Look, it's there."

She slid between two rocks, and he followed. In moments they were looking at the opening of a cave.

"Shiver me timbers," he said, and she laughed.

"Do you like pirate stories?" she asked.

"I've read some," he said. "I read Stevenson's *Treasure Island.*"

"I love that book," she said. "What about Blackbeard?"

"I've read some stuff about him, too."

"Well," she said, "now you'll likely be stepping where he once stood."

"Lead the way," he said.

Chapter Eight

They entered the cave.

The ground beneath them was wet and muddy, except where it was rock, then it was wet and slippery.

"How far back is it?" he asked.

"Not so far that we'll need a torch," she said. "At least, as long as it's light out."

Clint noticed that it was light in the cave. As he looked around he saw openings in the ceiling, through which the sun was streaming.

"The sun comes in enough to light the interior," she told him, "but not enough to dry it."

She slipped and he grabbed her around the waist to steady her.

"Thank you," she said.

"Here," he said, and took her hand.

She held his tightly.

"It's just a little bit further," she told him, and they continued, hand-in-hand.

Then she said, "There!"

Clint looked where she was pointing. It was a large, open area which had been dug up, at one point.

"That hole?"

"That's where the guns were found buried," she told him.

He looked round, saw remnants of the last high tide around them. It was entirely believable that the tide either brought the pieces in, or simply uncovered them.

"As I saw them, those pieces are very clean," he commented.

"Yes, after a team uncovered them they cleaned them ferociously until; they gleamed."

"And there's nothing left, right?" Clint asked.

"Right," she said. "They've now been through this entire cave, and found nothing else except some unre-markable remains of a ship," she said, "they'll use in the display."

"Are they all wood?"

"Some metal, some wood."

Clint looked around the cave again, and then decided he had done all he could there.

"All right," he said, "let's head back."

"Yes," she said, "now you have to get cleaned up for your supper with Miss Kennedy." She did not sound happy.

She led Clint back along the beach to the buggy.

"I better get you back to your Miss Kennedy in one piece," she said, as they climbed into the buggy.

"Why do I get the feeling there's more to this dislike?" he asked.

"You mean having her take my job isn't enough?"

"It sounds more personal than even that," he said, as they pulled away. "Are you sure she didn't take a man away from you, or something like that?"

"Oh? And who would that be? Mr. Fairchild? Please!"

Clint didn't comment.

"You think that amazon woman could take a man away from me?" she demanded.

"I don't know," he said. "I guess that would depend on the man."

"What about you?" she asked,

Carefully, he asked, "What about me?"

"Who would you rather be with?" she asked. "I mean, carnally. Me or Jayne Kennedy?"

"Well—"

"Never mind," she said, angrily, "you haven't seen me at my best. And she'll probably be all dressed up to take you to supper."

Charlotte grew quiet and didn't speak for the rest of the drive. Then Clint realized she wasn't taking him back to Fairchild's house, but to her place.

"I thought you'd be dropping me back at your boss' house."

39

"No," she said, "I'm still working, so I have to change back into my business clothes."

"Oh," he said, "okay."

"I can't let Mr. Fairchild see me like this," she said. "He'll think I was slacking off on his time."

"No fear of that," Clint said. "I'll tell him—"

"No!" she said, cutting him off. "I have to change."

They rode the rest of the way in silence, until she pulled the buggy to a stop in front of her building.

"Come up with me," she said, as they climbed down from the buggy.

"I can wait here again—"

"No," she said, "it's going to take me longer, this time. You better come up and I'll give you a drink while you wait."

"All right," he said. "However, you want to do it."

He followed her up the stairs to the second floor, where he found three large rooms—a kitchen, a living-room and a bedroom. She also had indoor running water.

"I can give you wine, sherry—but I know you don't like those."

"I'll just have some water," he said.

"We can do that," Charlotte said. She went to the kitchen and came back with a glass of water for him. "Now, just have a seat. I won't be long."

He sat down with the water and she went into her bed-room and closed the door.

After ten minutes he put the glass down, stood and walked to the window to look out. He could see the horse and buggy, and nothing else. It was obviously a quiet neighborhood.

He was thinking about the Blackbeard pieces when he heard Charlotte's voice.

"Clint, can you help me with this."

Thinking she needed help with a button or a boot he said, "Sure," and turned.

She was standing in the doorway of the bedroom. Stark naked.

Chapter Nine

"Charlotte . . ." he said, his mouth going dry.

She was a slender woman, with small, perfectly formed breasts that looked like ripe peaches. Her skin was smooth, the brown hair between her thighs was bushy, more plentiful even than the short hair on her pretty head.

"Charlotte," he tried again, after licking his lips, "what are you doing?"

"I just thought," she said, posing in the doorway, "since Jayne Kennedy was obviously going to try to charm the pants off you, that I would beat her to it."

"Look, I'm only going to have a meal with her—"

"Well then," she said, cutting him off, "here I am, completely naked. What are you going to do with me?"

"It's getting pretty late," he said, "and I do have an appointment with Miss Kennedy."

"And you need me to drive you back to Fairchild's house so you can get ready," she reminded him. She walked over to him and placed her hand on his chest. "The sooner you give me what I want, the sooner you get what you want."

Now that she was close he could feel the heat of her naked skin. Her firm breasts with their tasty looking brown nipples were right in front of his face, and he didn't have much choice. His body was responding.

"Okay," he said, "you win."

He grabbed her, pulled her to him, kissed her soundly, then lifted her in his arms and carried her back into the bedroom. He didn't take the time to look the room over but went right to the bed. Without even getting undressed he dropped her onto her back, grabbed her legs, spread them, got down on his knees and pressed his face to her crotch. It was already wet and fragrant, and he drove his tongue into that wetness.

He worked her that way until she was writhing on the bed wetting the bedclothes beneath her—and Clint's face—copiously. Only then, after waves of pleasure washed over her, leaving her almost exhausted, did he stand, undress and join her on the bed.

In spite of the fact that she was still trying to regain her breath, she reached for him as he once again spread her legs, this time driving his hard cock into her, brutally. This was what she wanted, so he was going to enjoy it, thoroughly. And maybe after giving her what she wanted, she would talk to him more freely about her employer's business.

So this was for pleasure and, at the same time, for his benefit.

As he continued to pound at her, she implored him for more, bringing her hips up to meet his every thrust. This was not the young woman he had met at the train station. That one had seemed meek and gentle. This woman was hungry, passionate, and demanding. And although he had assumed control from the start, he had the feeling she was still somehow directing the action. And, if she could do so even under these physical circumstances, why had she had trouble getting Fairchild to keep his promise?

He began to grunt with the effort as his own explosion approached, and she cried out loudly as he finally erupted inside of her. Together, they slumped on the mattress, catching their breath.

"Give me a minute or two," she finally said, "and I'll drive you back. You can have your steak with Miss Kennedy now but be thinking of me while you sit across from her."

"I'll be thinking about this, all right," he told her. "You can be sure of that."

She smiled, then laughed and said, "Good."

***

It took longer than a few minutes, but finally they walked to the horse and buggy together, Charlotte back in her work clothes and looking quite demure. They sat side-by-side on the driver's seat as she directed the horses to the Fairchild house.

"I'm going to assume that Walter Fairchild doesn't know the Charlotte Goodrich I just met."

"No one around here does," she said. "I keep that Charlotte down deep inside."

"Then why was I lucky enough to meet her?" Clint asked.

"Every once in a while I need to release my hold on her," Charlotte said. "I can't very well do that with someone who lives around here, someone I might see every day. You'll only be here long enough to authenticate those guns."

"Well," he said, "then I was a lucky man today."

She laughed.

"And not only today, if you play your cards right."

***

She pulled up in front of the house and said, "There you go."

"Are you coming in?" he asked.

"No," she said, "I feel in need of a bath before I actually go back to work. Please tell Mr. Fairchild I did my job today, and I'll see you both in the morning."

"I'll tell him you did your job," he said, stepping down, "even though you did a lot more than that."

"And enjoy your time with Miss Kennedy," she said, snapping the reins at the horse, "if you can."

Chapter Ten

"There you are!" Walter Fairchild exclaimed as Clint entered the house. "Where did you and Charlotte get off to?"

"I had her take me to the caves."

"Oh? What for?"

"I just wanted a look, and to get a feel of where the pieces were found."

"I hear you're going to supper with Jayne tonight."

"That's right," Clint said, "and I need to get cleaned up and changed. Not that I have the kind of clothes I might need for supper around here."

"Is she taking you for a steak?"

"That's the plan."

"I have an idea of where she might be taking you," he said. "Anything you wear will be fine."

"Thanks," Clint said.

"If you get back late tonight, I'll see you in the morning. After breakfast, I'll take you to actually inspect the pieces."

"I'm looking forward to that."

He went upstairs to use the facilities and get himself ready for Jayne Kennedy.

He cleaned up as well as he could without taking a bath. When he was satisfied that he no longer smelled of the cave, or of Charlotte, he got dressed and went downstairs to wait for Jayne Kennedy.

He was outside on the front porch when she pulled up in a buggy. The driver helped her down and she walked toward him, wearing a long blue dress. Her blonde hair was hanging past her shoulders.

"I'm underdressed," he said. He was once again wearing his jacket, to cover the gun on his hip. Other than that he simply had clean trail clothes beneath it.

"Not at all," she said. "I just like to get out of my business clothes every once in a while. Shall we go?"

"Definitely."

He walked to the buggy with her, helped her into the back seat while the driver climbed into his seat.

"Let's go!" she called when Clint was seated beside her. She looked at him. "How did your day go with Charlotte?"

"It was fine."

"Did she show you everything?"

"Everything?"

Jayne nodded.

"The beach, the caves, where the guns came from?"

"Ah, yes," he said. "She showed me all of that."

"And?"

"And I'm anxious to hold the actual guns of Blackbeard, in my hands."

"And then you'll decide whether or not they are Blackbeard's guns, eh?"

"I will."

They rode silently for a few minutes, and then Jayne asked, "What else did Charlotte tell you?"

"What else is there?" he asked.

She laughed.

"Did she tell you how I stole her job?"

"She, uh, might have mentioned something about that."

Jayne laughed, again. Sitting next to her he could feel the firmness, the power of her, and he could smell the sweetness of her.

"Did she tell you that I was more qualified for the job than she was?"

"No, she didn't."

"Let me guess," Jayne said. "She told you I charmed Fairchild into giving me the job."

"Actually," Clint answered, "she said you charmed the pants off him."

"Typical," Jayne said.

"Can you have her fired?" Clint asked. "Do you have that much power?"

49

"No," she said. "I run the museum. She works for Mr. Fairchild. He can fire her, or me. She and I have no control over each other."

"I see."

"So she and I," Jayne said, "we're just stuck with each other."

***

When the buggy stopped in front of a restaurant Jayne smiled at Clint.

"The best steak in North Carolina," she told him. "You'll see."

"I can't wait."

He got out first, and then helped her.

"Two hours," she told the driver.

"Yes, Miss." He was a young man, and the way he looked at her Clint had no doubt he was in love with her, even though she was almost 20 years older than he was.

"Come," she said, taking Clint's arm, "they're holding a table for us."

Chapter Eleven

The table being held for them was a private one, walled off from the rest of the large diningroom. A maître d' showed them to it, and Jayne immediately ordered a bottle of wine.

"I hope you don't mind," she said.

Instead of telling her he wasn't a wine drinker, he said, "Not at all. In fact, I'll leave you to order the food, as well, since you know the place. And they seem to know you."

The other diners in the room had turned to look at them as they entered. Clint was used to that, but this wasn't the West, and he knew they were looking at Jayne, not him. Some of them even greeted her as the two followed the maître d' across the room.

"I eat here quite often," she said. "And many of these people come to the museum."

When the waiter came with the wine Jayne waited until he was finished pouring and then ordered two steak platters "with all the trimmings, please, Peter."

"Of course, Miss," the waiter said.

They both sipped the wine, which Clint told her was "fine."

When the steak came it was more than fine. It was everything she said it would be. So were the trimmings.

For a large woman, Jayne ate with a dainty hand, but devoured her entire plateful. The appetite belied her manners.

"I'm sorry," she said, when she finished her meal. "I was very hungry."

"No apology needed for having a good appetite," he said, pushing his empty plate away. "I did the same."

"You didn't drink your wine," she said. "I think I know why." She waved to the waiter. When he arrived she said, "Will you please bring Mr. Adams a cold mug of beer."

The waiter nodded and went to fetch it.

When he returned and set it on the table, Clint said, "Thank you."

He picked it up and drank half of it down.

"I should've known," Jayne said, "and ordered you a beer from the start. After all, you're a Westerner."

"Actually," he said, "I was born in the East, migrated to the West at an early age. But I have never had a taste for wine."

"Well, how's the beer?"

"It's great," he said. "Nice and cold."

"You can have another with dessert."

"Pie?" he asked.

"All kinds," she answered. "What do you like?"

"Peach is my favorite."

"Peach it is. With another beer?"

"Coffee," he said. "Black and strong."

She called Peter over again and gave him their order—peach pie for him, cherry for her. Coffee for both.

"So," she said, "are you excited about tomorrow?"

"Very," he said. "I can't wait for those pieces to be in my hands."

"But," she said, "what if they're not real?"

"Well," he said, "then we'll all be disappointed, won't we?"

"Unless . . ."

"Unless what?"

She smiled at him, put her elbow on the table and her chin in her hand.

"Unless no matter what," she replied, "you say they're real, and we open the museum."

He sat back.

"Is that what you want me to do?" he asked. "Lie?"

"I only want you to lie," she said, "if you have to."

"And does your employer know about this?" he asked. "That you're asking me to do this?"

"Oh, no," she said. "I make my own decisions about my own actions, Clint."

"So do I," Clint said. "I'm going to examine those pieces and then tell Fairchild what I find."

"Not me?"

"He's paying me," Clint said. "In fact, he's paying all of us, isn't he? Me, Charlotte and you."

"I'm paid by the board," Jayne said, "but yes, technically the money is coming from him."

"Well," Clint said, "I don't know anything about the board. I just know that Fairchild brought me here to do a job, and I'm going to do it." He sat forward as the waiter brought the pie. "Is that a problem for you?"

"No," she said, looking at her own pie. "It's not."

"And if I lied for you," Clint asked, "what would you be offering in return?"

She smiled.

"Since you've already told me you won't lie," she asked, "what would be the point of answering that question?"

***

Jayne had the buggy drive Clint back to Fairchild's house after supper. He had been wondering about Charlotte's comment, that Jayne had "charmed the pants off of," Fairchild. After she asked him to lie, he wondered if she was going to try to do the same to him. But instead, she took him right back to the big house.

He considered asking her flat out if she was sleeping with Fairchild but decided against it. First, he had to decide whether or not he should tell his host about Jayne's offer.

Chapter Twelve

Clint slept well, after travelling that day before, exploring the caves, and spending time with both Charlotte and Jayne. He came down to the diningroom for breakfast and found Walter Fairchild sitting alone, in shirtsleeves.

"Good morning," he greeted.

"Good morning, Mr. Adams."

"Please," Clint said, sitting across from the man, "call me Clint."

"And you can call me Walter," Fairchild said.

The cook came out then and stood patiently.

"Just tell cook what you want, and she'll prepare it for you," Fairchild said.

"Anything?" Clint asked.

"Yes, anything."

Clint looked at the woman.

"It's been a while since I had a stack of good buttermilk flapjacks," he said.

"Then you'll have it. And coffee?"

"Yes, coffee," Clint said.

"Cook, flapjacks and coffee for both of us."

The cook nodded and left the room.

"So," Fairchild said, "how was your supper with Jayne?"

"It was very good," Clint said. "You know the place she took us? There was no name out front."

"Carlyle's," Fairchild said. "He owns it but doesn't want his name on the building."

"But everyone knows it's his?"

"Oh, yes, everyone knows."

"Like everyone knows you run the museum?"

"The museum is run by the board," Fairchild said, "with Jayne Kennedy seeing to the everyday operations."

"Yes," Clint said, "but most of the money is coming from you, right?"

"Is that what Jayne told you?"

"No," Clint lied, "it's what I assumed."

"I do sit at the head of the board," Fairchild admitted, "but all the decisions are made as a group."

"I see."

"But it was my decision to bring you here," Fairchild admitted, "and I'm the one who's paying you."

"And you pay Charlotte?"

"Yes."

"And the board pays Jayne."

"Correct."

"But you are her boss."

"This is all true," Fairchild said.

The cook came out with a coffee pot and poured for both of them, then went back to the kitchen. Clint heard the front door open and close, and then Charlotte entered the diningroom.

"Good morning, Charlotte," Fairchild said.

"Good morning, sir," she said. "Good morning, Clint."

"Morning," Clint said. "Flapjacks?"

"Is that what we're having?" she asked.

"Yes."

"Then flapjacks it is."

She started to sit, but Fairchild told her, "You'd better go and tell cook you're here."

"Yes," she said, "I will."

She went into the kitchen, came right back out again and sat with the two men.

"What are we talking about?" she asked.

"I was talking to your boss about just who is boss around here," Clint said.

"And what did he say?"

"He told me the board rules," Clint said, "but that he has the money. And do you know what that means to me?"

"What?" she asked.

"The man with the money is the boss."

The cook came out of the kitchen with the flapjacks.

After breakfast Fairchild went to his room and said he would be down to take Clint to the museum.

Once he was gone Charlotte asked, "What did you tell him about what we did yesterday."

"We went to see the caves, and the pieces, and I met Jayne."

"And had supper with her."

"Yes."

They were waiting for Fairchild in the livingroom. Charlotte came closer to him.

"And did you tell him what else we did yesterday?"

"Some things," he told her, "are just between you and me."

"Yes," she said.

They were kissing when they heard Fairchild coming down the stairs. When he entered the room, they were at different ends of it. Fairchild was wearing a three piece suit.

"Are we ready to go and take a look at those pieces?" he asked.

"Ready," Clint said, "and eager."

"Do we have a buggy with a driver?" he asked Charlotte.

"We do, sir."

"Then let's not waste any more time."

Chapter Thirteen

The driver dropped the three of them off in the front of the museum, this time, rather than at the back door Charlotte had taken him to the day before.

"Just hang around, Paul," Fairchild told the man. "I'm not sure when we'll be needing you again."

"Sure, boss."

Fairchild led the way to the front door, which he opened with a key—a key Charlotte obviously didn't have.

"Let's go to Jayne's office," he said, "and I'll have the pieces brought there."

"Who's going to touch them?" Clint asked.

"I'll have the entire display case brought in," Fairchild said. "That way you'll be the only one touching them."

"That'll work."

He followed Fairchild to Jayne's office, with Charlotte bringing up the rear. She obviously was not very happy. But he hadn't had a chance to ask her why.

Fairchild knocked on Jayne Kennedy's door before opening it. As they entered she looked up from her desk, frowned, and then smiled.

"Good morning Walter, Clint," Jayne said. He hesitated before saying, "Charlotte."

"Morning," Fairchild said. "Can we have the display case brought here for Clint?"

"Of course," Jayne said, coming out from behind her desk. "I'll see to it."

"It would be nice to have some coffee, as well."

"Coming right up."

Jayne left the room to see to her boss' wishes. Clint felt his request for coffee was his way of flexing his muscles at her.

"Have a seat," Fairchild said to Clint.

There were many chairs in the room, and off to one side a long table lined with wooden chairs. For meetings with the board, he assumed.

He chose an armchair that faced Jayne's desk, and sat. Charlotte sat in a chair next to him.

He watched Fairchild, wondering if the man would take Jayne's desk, as another show of his superiority. But he did not. Instead, he remained standing.

A young girl brought in a tray with a coffee pot and cups first, filled them for everyone and handed them out.

"Thank you," Clint said.

"You're welcome."

The girl smiled. She couldn't have been more than 15. She turned and left the room.

Clint, Charlotte and Fairchild drank their coffee, and waited.

***

When Jayne Kennedy left the office, she found the 15 year old girl whose name was Lacy, and told her to bring coffee to Mr. Fairchild and his guests.

"Yes, Ma'am."

Then she found two workmen and said, "We must carry the Blackbeard display case to my office, where they will be examined."

"Yes, Ma'am," the two men said. They were both young, in their early 20s, and she knew they would do anything she asked them to do. It had always been that way for her with men, ever since she was a teenager and her breasts swelled. As she got older, the rest of her body caught up, and her hair became as golden as the sun.

"Carry it in," she said, "carefully."

"Miss Kennedy," one of them asked, "do you still want us to kill Mr. Fairchild?"

"When did I ever say that?" she demanded.

"In your office," he said, "when we were both having sex with you, you said—"

"Forget that ever happened!" she snapped. It had been a weak moment for her, taking the virginity of both young men. She had been drinking, and talking too much, and perhaps there had been things she'd said that she didn't remember saying.

"Just carry the display into my office, and then leave," she said. "Do you understand?"

"Yes, Miss."

As she left them the two young men exchanged a glance, shrugged, and then headed for the display case, where she was waiting to supervise.

***

When the door opened again Clint saw two men carrying the display case with the guns inside. Behind them came Jayne Kennedy.

"Over there," she said, pointing. "Next to the long table."

They carried it across the room and set it down next to the long conference table.

"That's all," she told them. "Thank you, boys."

Clint saw the way the boys looked at her. He wondered if, in a room with just the two of them, she affected Walter Fairchild this way?

Then he forgot all about them, and that question, and walked over to the display case.

Chapter Fourteen

"Who has the key?" Clint asked, looking down at the guns through the glass.

"Mr. Fairchild has that," Jayne said.

"Here," Fairchild said, stepping forward, "let me unlock it."

He took the key from the pocket of his vest, fitted it into the lock and turned it.

"There you go."

Clint slid the glass aside, and now there was nothing between him, the flintlock and the blunderbuss.

Fairchild, Charlotte and Jayne remained behind him, saying nothing.

Clint picked up the flintlock first. The story went that Blackbeard had it made especially for him, and that it was one of six he wore at the same time.

The double-barrel Flintlock came to prominence following the French and Indian War, around 1760. If Blackbeard had this one build in 1717, then he pretty much invented the thing more than 40 years earlier.

It was an exquisite piece of work, but whether or not it belonged to Blackbeard was not something he could tell at this early stage.

He set the flintlock down and picked up the blunder-buss, next. The earliest version of the shotgun did not need shells in order to wreak havoc on the human body. A handful of nails, or pebbles, could be shoved down the barrel, and when fired they would become deadly, tearing into flesh and bone, alike.

He rotated the weapon, once again—as with the flint-lock—noticing the excellent workmanship. Whoever had built these guns was a master, indeed.

"So?" Fairchild asked, as Clint set the blunderbuss down. "Are they his?"

"I'm afraid that's not something I could tell you right now," Clint answered. "I need to examine them more closely, using my tools."

"Using your tools?" Fairchild asked, puzzled.

"I'm not only called The Gunsmith—" He turned, looked at Fairchild. "—I am one."

***

Fairchild continued to apologize profusely.

"I'm so sorry," he said, again. "I only know your rep-utation. I didn't know that you were actually a . . . a tradesman."

"I gave it up many years ago," Clint admitted, "but I can still use a bell sander or a brass hammer."

"Of course, of course . . ." Fairchild said.

"I don't have my own, however," Clint said. "You'll have to get me a kit, something basic."

"Yes, yes, I'll get on that right away," Fairchild said. "There's a gunsmith in town. But . . . at first glance what do you think?"

"I think," Clint said, "it looks very promising."

"Oh, excellent," Fairchild said, "that's excellent news."

"But those are not my findings, yet."

"No, of course not."

Clint looked at Jayne.

"Would it be possible for me to work in here?" he asked. "Keep the display case here, locked?"

"Yes, of course," she said. "Whatever you need."

"And the doors will be kept locked, as well?" he asked.

"They always are," Jayne Kennedy said.

"Good." Clint looked at Fairchild. "Do you have any security, at all?"

"Of course," the man said. "We have men on duty at night."

"I'll need to meet them," Clint said.

"That can be arranged."

"And the day men, as well."

"Day men?"

"I assume you have security men on duty during the day," Clint said.

"Well, no . . ." Fairchild said.

"Walter," Clint said, patiently, "we're really going to have to talk."

"Yes, yes," Fairchild said, "of course." He turned. "Charlotte, please arrange for the security men we do have, to be available to Clint."

"Yes, sir."

"And," Clint said, "we'll be looking to hire some new men, as well."

"Right. I can get them from town—"

"I'll want to interview them," Clint said, cutting Fairchild off, "and after that, and a conversation with your night men, I'll let you know who's staying, who's leaving, and who's hiring on."

"You won't be hiring and firing museum personnel, as well, will you?" Jayne asked him.

He looked at her.

"I'll need to talk to them," he said, "and then . . . who knows?"

Chapter Fifteen

Jayne agreed to bring the security men into her office when they arrived. Meanwhile, Clint wanted to walk around the entire museum, look at all the doors and windows. Charlotte decided to walk with him.

"Do you see what she's doing?" Charlotte asked.

"Hmm? Who?"

"Jayne!" Charlotte said. "Don't you see the way she controls the men around her?"

"You mean those two workmen?"

"Them, Fairchild . . . even you, for all I know."

Clint had been studying a window, turned to look at her.

"The only woman around here who's had any control over me is you," he said, "or don't you remember?"

She giggled and said, "I do remember, very well. But you can bet Jayne's going to try with you."

"She's already asked me to lie," Clint said.

"About what?"

"The Blackbeard guns. She wants me to say they're his, whether they are or not."

Her eyes went wide.

"Did you tell Mr. Fairchild?"

"No, not yet."

"Why not? He'd fire her on the spot."

"You think so?" Clint asked.

"You don't?"

"Well, first of all, you're claiming she controls him. Second, I'm not sure he doesn't already know."

"You think Mr. Fairchild would condone lying about the pieces?" she asked.

"I think everybody seems to be relying on them being real," Clint said.

"So what are you going to do?"

"I'm going to do the job I was hired to do," Clint said. "Prove or disprove that they were Blackbeard's guns."

"And what about security?"

"I'm checking door and window locks," Clint said, "but a place like this needs security day and night. The men you hire will be important."

"Not me," Charlotte said. "Those men were hired by Mr. Fairchild and Jayne."

"I think I'd depend more on your choices than theirs," Clint said.

"I appreciate that," she said.

"Let's finish with the doors and then see if Jayne has brought her men in."

***

Jayne had two men in her office, wearing dark clothes and a gunbelt.

"This is Clint Adams." she told them. "He's been hired to check our security."

"I know that name," one of them said, "but I thought it was a, uh, legend."

"The Gunsmith?" the other man said. "He *is* a legend." The second man looked at Clint. "This is a real pleasure."

"I hope you still feel that way when we're done here," Clint said. "Sit down."

"Do you want some privacy?" Jayne asked.

"No," Clint said, "you and Charlotte can stay."

The two women stared daggers at each other.

Clint questioned both men, whose named were Coates and Dabney. He didn't keep them long, and finally sent them back to work.

"So?" Jayne asked. "What did you think."

"Coates can stay," Clint said. The man was in his 40s and had some experience. The other one, Dabney, was in his 30s and Clint didn't like him. He didn't seem to take anything, seriously. "Dabney has to go."

"Why?" Jayne asked.

"He's not serious enough about his job."

"How can you tell?" Jayne asked.

"His answers," Clint said, "and the gun he's wearing on his hip."

"We told the security men they had to provide their own weapons."

"Well, his is terrible," Clint said.

"So what do I do? Fire him?"

"Yes, but not right away," he told her. "Let's wait until we have a replacement."

"Fine."

"We'll have to interview some men for that spot, as well as the nights."

"And I think Coates should be put in charge."

"I don't care about that," Jayne said.

"I'll talk to Mr. Fairchild," Charlotte said.

"Sure," Jayne said, "let Charlotte do it. She can get the old man to do anything."

"Fine," Clint said. That was pretty much what Charlotte had said about Jayne. He looked at the two women, then at the once again locked display case. "I think I'm done for the day. Just be sure that thing is locked away."

"Don't worry," Jayne said. "We'll use the two security men we have to keep it safe until we get more."

He looked at Charlotte.

"I need you to get me to the telegraph office."

"That's in town," she said. "Let's go now, or they'll close before we get there." Charlotte looked at Jayne but spoke to Clint. "We can get supper while we're at it."

"That suits me," Clint said. "Jayne, we'll see you tomorrow."

"Enjoy your supper," she said.

As he and Charlotte headed for the door Clint said, "Feel free to tell Mr. Fairchild where we went."

"I'll do that," the curator said.

***

In the buggy Charlotte and Clint sat in the back while the driver took them to the telegraph office.

"That bitch!" Charlotte said.

"She seems like an efficient woman," Clint said.

"Yes," Charlotte said, "she's very efficiently getting her way and doing my job."

Chapter Sixteen

The town of Ocracoke was a small, seaside town, but was growing. And one of the things that was helping it grow was the telegraph office.

"Ever since they put the telegraph in, more and more businesses are opening," Charlotte told him.

"Including the museum?"

"Yes, that's one of the reasons they opened the museum," she said. "You can see that the building used to be a mansion where people lived, but Mr. Fairchild bought it and turned it into the museum."

The buggy pulled up in front of the telegraph office.

"How long will you be?" she asked.

"I'm not sure," he said. "I'm going to send a few, some of which might come back to me right away."

"Well, since we're in town I'm going to do some shopping," she said.

"Go ahead," he said, helping her down. "I'll be here whenever you get back."

"There's a restaurant down the street I want to take you to," she said.

"Great. By the time you get back, I'll be hungry."

Clint went into the office, while Charlotte turned and walked up the street. The driver was left to his own devices.

"Help ya?" the telegraph clerk asked.

"I need to send a few telegrams," Clint said. "If you'll give me the paper and pencil, I'll sit over there and get them written out."

"They gonna be long ones?" he asked, passing Clint what he needed.

"Probably longer than usual," Clint admitted.

"Well," the clerk said, "I was about to go out and get somethin' to eat. It shouldn't take long. I'm gonna bring it back here."

"That's fine," Clint said. "This will probably take me a while."

"Great!" the young man said, happily. "I'll be right back."

Clint sat at a desk against the wall and started to write.

He was on the third telegram when he heard somebody enter the office. Without turning he knew at least three people were there, looking at him.

"Clerk around?" a man asked.

"No," Clint said, "but he'll be right back. He went to get something to eat."

"Looks like you're gonna have a lot of work for him when he gets back."

"He'll handle it," Clint said.

"Why don't you let us see what you're writin', there?" the voice asked.

That was when Clint turned to look. Three men were standing just inside the door, wearing shirts, jeans and jackets, and he had the distinct impression of guns beneath the jackets.

"I told you fellas the clerk will be back soon," he said. "Why don't you go somewhere and get a drink, and come back?"

"We ain't thirsty," the man standing in the center said. They were big beefy men, who probably did more damage with their fists than their guns.

"Well then, go get a snack," Clint said. "I'm busy."

"Yeah, we heard," the man said. "You been up to that ritzy museum."

"Who the hell are you?" Clint asked.

The man shrugged.

"Just three curious fellas," he said, "wonderin' what a fella like you is doin' around here."

"Just visiting," Clint said.

"Visitin'?" the man asked. "Caves?"

If these three men had followed him and Charlotte to the caves, Clint was concerned, because he never saw them.

Chapter Seventeen

"You fellas want to fill me in on your interest in me?" Clint asked.

"We heard some talk about Blackbeard the Pirate," the middle man said.

"What about him?"

"We work for a man who would pay a lot of money for those guns," the man said. "The flintlock and the blunderpuss."

"Buss," one of the other men said, correcting him, "blunderbuss."

"Right, that one," the middle man said.

"What's your name?" Clint asked him.

"I'm Pete Anderson," the man said, "this is—"

"I don't care about them," Clint said, cutting him off, "you're the one doing the talking. Go back and tell the man you work for to make his offer to the proper people at the museum."

"He's thinkin' he can get a cheaper price from you," Anderson said.

"Then he's thinking wrong," Clint said.

"What if we press you for it?" Anderson asked.

"Then you tell your boss that sending the three of you against me is going to cost him more than he can imagine."

Clint had no idea if the men knew his name.

"And who should I tell him is sending him this message?" Anderson asked.

Well, that answered the name question.

"My name is Clint Adams."

The three men stared at him.

"Adams?" one of the others asked.

"That's right."

He nudged Anderson, hard.

"I know, I know!" Anderson said.

Suddenly, all three men made sure their hands were in plain view.

"Okay," Anderson said, "we'll tell 'im."

The three men backed out of the office, almost with their hands in the air, as if Clint was actually holding a gun on them.

Seconds later the clerk came back in.

"What happened?" he asked. "Who were those men?"

"Oh, they were looking for you," Clint told him, "said they had a message to send."

"Why'd they leave?"

"I guess they changed their minds," Clint said.

The clerk took what looked like a sandwich behind the counter with him.

"It looked like they had their hands up," he commented.

"Did it?"

"Are you ready with those?"

"Not yet," Clint said. "Eat your sandwich. I'll let you know when."

The clerk unwrapped his sandwich and took a huge bite.

***

When Clint had the telegrams ready he went up to the counter, where the clerk still had half his sandwich left.

"Ready?" the young man asked.

"Yes," Clint said. "I have three."

He passed them over.

"Are you expecting quick replies?" the clerk asked.

"Possibly," Clint said. "I'm going to be at a restaurant that's up the street from here."

"Which one?" the clerk asked. "There's three."

"I'm not sure," Clint said. "Can you check all three to see if I'm there?"

"I dunno," the clerk said. "I'm here alone—"

"I'll make it worth your while," Clint promised.

"This is just to start," Clint said, handing the young man a couple of dollars.

"Well, okay," the man said, accepting the money. He looked at the telegrams. "Denver, Philadelphia and New York?"

"That's right."

Clint turned as someone entered the office and saw that it was Charlotte.

"Charlotte," Clint said, "I'm glad to see you."

"I'm glad to see you, too."

"Can you please tell this young man what restaurant we're going to be in?"

"Yes, of course," she said. "Patsy's."

"Hey," the clerk said, "that place is pretty good. Okay, if a reply comes in I'll bring it over to Patsy's."

"Thanks," Clint said.

As Clint and Charlotte stepped outside she asked, "Are you expecting responses that soon?"

"I hope so," he said, "from at least one of them."

"This way," she said, taking his arm and guiding him up the street.

"I thought you were going shopping?" he asked, observing that her hands were empty.

"I had my packages put in the buggy, which is parked in front of Patsy's."

As they reached the restaurant he saw the buggy, but there was no driver.

"He's gone to get something to eat, himself," she said.

"Inside?"

"No," she said, "Patsy's is too expensive for a driver."

As they turned to enter he saw the restaurant Jayne had taken him to, Carlyle's, was right across the street.

Chapter Eighteen

Patsy's was very similar to Carlyle's in almost every respect, except that it did have the name above the door, and etched into the window. The clientele looked to be the same class, as did the menu.

"Would you like me to order for both of us?" Charlotte asked. "I mean, since I've been here before."

"Please," Clint said, "go ahead."

She waved a waiter over and ordered two steak dinners. Clint saw that he was going to be able to compare, steak-o-steak, between the two restaurants.

Charlotte showed a little more knowledge of what Clint liked, as she ordered wine for herself, but a mug of beer for him.

"I'll bet Jayne took you across the street," she said, as the waiter moved away, "but I think this place is better."

"It'll be interesting," he said, wondering if he should be truthful?

"Don't worry," she said, as if reading his mind, "you can tell the truth."

He smiled and wished he had his beer.

***

The steaks were delivered to the table, and Clint knew from the first bite that Carlyle's beef was better. Or their cook was. What was he supposed to say?

"So who did you send those telegrams to?" Charlotte asked.

Clint welcomed the questions, which took the attention away from the steaks.

"Some friends of mine."

"About what?"

"Blackbeard's guns."

"Why? Do you need help?"

"Obviously," he said. "And while Fairchild is getting me that gunsmithing kit, maybe I can get some."

"From who?"

"Experts."

"In a telegram?"

"Two of them are in the East," Clint said. "Philadelphia and New York. They can be here quickly."

"So you're saying you can't authenticate these pieces?"

"No one can do that alone," Clint said. "I'll need at least one expert to agree with me."

"One of the three people you contacted?"

"Yes."

"And who pays them?"

"They'll do it as a favor to me," Clint said, "and to see the pieces."

"And will you tell Fairchild about this?"

"Sure," Clint said, "the more experts agree, the better for him."

"I suppose." She pushed her plate away. "Dessert?"

"You order that, too."

***

After coffee and cake, they left Patsy's and climbed back aboard the buggy.

"Mr. Adams! Mr. Adams!"

"Just when I thought it was too late," Clint said, as the telegraph clerk ran up to them.

"You got three replies," the young man said. "I was so surprised."

"Thank you," Clint said, and handed the man another dollar for each reply.

"Thank you!"

"What do they say?" Charlotte asked.

"I thought I'd read them when I got back to my room," Clint said.

"Our driver's not here, yet," she said. "We've got to have something to do."

"All right," Clint said. "This one is from a man I knew in New York, who worked for P.T. Barnum."

"What's he say?"

Clint read it quietly, then folded it.

"He's told me some small details to look for on the guns, that would authenticate them."

"That's very helpful!"

"Yes, it is."

"What about another one?"

"This is from a friend of mine in Philadelphia," Clint told her. "He's an expert on guns."

"What's he say?"

Clint read, and smiled.

"He's already on his way here," he said, folding the telegram. "We'll need to find him a hotel."

"You don't want him to stay at Fairchild's?"

"I don't think so."

"Then," she said. "I think I have just the place."

"Nothing too cheap."

"Of course not."

"And the third telegram?"

He looked at the one from Denver, which was from Talbot Roper.

"I'll read that one in my room," he said. "Here comes our driver."

Chapter Nineteen

The driver took them back to the house, where Clint stepped out.

"I'm going home," Charlotte told him. "You sure you don't want to come with me?"

"I need to talk with Walter for a while," Clint said. "I'll see you tomorrow."

"Yes, you will," Charlotte said. She tapped the driver on the shoulder and off they went.

Clint went into the house, which was quiet. He wondered why Fairchild didn't seem to have any staff except for the cook? But his bed got made, so there must have been somebody there for that. And the house was always clean.

He checked the diningroom, found no one there, then stuck his head in the kitchen. The cook—who Fairchild simply called "cook,"—turned from the sink and looked at him, arms folded across her chest.

"I'm looking for Walter."

"Mr. Fairchild is in his library," she said.

"Thank you."

He went back through the entry hall to the other side of the house, followed a hallway to the door of Fairchild's library. The man was sitting in an armchair, holding a glass of sherry, or port.

"Good evening, Clint," Fairchild said. "I'd offer you a glass of sherry, but I know it's not to your taste. I'm sorry I have no beer, here."

"That's fine."

"I can have cook make some coffee."

"That would be fine. Should I go and tell her?"

"No," the man said, "it'll be done."

"I notice you don't have much staff for a house this size."

"I do have some," Fairchild said, "but part of their job is to be unobtrusive. They've been told to be seen only when I call for them."

"I see."

"How was your day with Blackbeard's guns?" Fairchild asked.

"Encouraging," Clint replied, "as I said earlier today. What about my tools?"

"They will be delivered in the morning."

"Then I can have a closer look."

"Excellent. Uh, any idea, then, how long before you can authenticate?"

"I ask you to give me a few more days."

"Days, eh?" Fairchild said. "Well, I suppose it pays to be patient." He stood up. "I'll see to the coffee. Be back in a moment."

He left, carrying his glass of sherry.

"Your coffee, sir," the cook said, appearing at the door with a tray.

"Thank you."

She set it down on a sideboard and turned to leave.

"Cook."

"Yes?"

"What other staff does Mr. Fairchild have in the house?" he asked.

"Two maids, and a man servant."

"Man servant?"

"He doesn't like to be called a butler."

"And do they live on the premises?"

"They do."

"And where—"

"I have to go," she said. "I have work. Mr. Fairchild can answer your questions."

"I guess he can," Clint said. "Thanks again for the coffee."

Cook started for the door, but stopped before leaving, and turned back.

"I'll tell you one thing," she said.

"What's that?"

"Don't trust that bitch, Jayne Kennedy."

"You don't like her?"

"Not at all," the cook said. "She's not what she seems to be."

"Can you be more spec—"

"No." She turned and left the room.

So, cook didn't like Jayne, and neither did Charlotte. Clint wondered if the tall blonde was just the kind of woman other females didn't like. Maybe they were . . . jealous of her? Or was there something else.

"Ah, you have your coffee," Fairchild said, entering the room. "I'll pour myself some more sherry and then we can toast our success."

"Why not?" Clint asked, picking up his cup.

"Are there any other eventualities I should know about?" Fairchild asked.

"Not yet," Clint said.

"But if there are, I'll be the first to know, right?" the man asked, turning with his glass full.

"You know you will," Clint said. "After all, you're paying the bills."

"Yes, I am."

Clint decided to hold back what he had told Charlotte about his other experts. It would be interesting to see whether or not she passed the information on to her employer.

"To Blackbeard's guns," Fairchild said.

"To Blackbeard's guns," Clint said, raising his coffee cup.

***

In his room Clint unfolded the reply to the third telegram he had sent, that one to Talbot Roper, in Denver. When he had met Walter Fairchild, he had actually been investigating the man, hired by the board. He hadn't found anything, but he told Clint to be careful. There was more to Fairchild then met the eye. That was all he had been able to put in the telegram. Except that he would come back if Clint needed him.

Clint refolded the telegram and put it in his carpetbag, with the others. He would send for Roper if he truly needed him, but he had help coming, and had already decided there was more to Fairchild than there appeared to be.

As for Jayne, there seemed to be more between her and Fairchild, just as there seemed to be something going on with Fairchild and Charlotte.

At the moment, Charlotte seemed to be his best bet for more information. He would start working on her the next day.

Chapter Twenty

In the morning Charlotte once again arrived for breakfast, but this time she sat silent while Clint and Fairchild discussed what would be coming that day.

And Clint told Fairchild one other thing.

"Walter, I think you're going to have to think a little harder about who might not want me here."

"Why is that?"

"I was approached by three beefy fellas who were looking for a fight," Clint said.

"Maybe they just knew who you were?" Fairchild said. "I mean, doesn't that kind of thing happen to you often?"

"In the West, yes, where men want to try their luck with a gun," Clint said. "These three were armed, but they were trying to intimidate me, physically."

"And?"

"And I think I ended up intimidating them when I introduced myself."

"They didn't say who they were representing?" Fairchild asked.

"Not a word."

"So you think this is the second attempt to . . . what? Scare you off?"

"Maybe," Clint said, "those three yesterday, but that young man at the train station, he was trying to take me somewhere."

"Well," Fairchild said, "if you see him again around town, you can ask him."

"You can bet I will," Clint said. "What about my kit?"

"It should be waiting for you at the museum."

"Then why don't we get going?" Clint said, standing up.

As they stood Fairchild said, "Not you, Charlotte."

"What?"

"I have something else for you to take care of," Fairchild said. "You can come by the museum later in the day."

"What is it?" she asked. "I thought you wanted me to look after Clint."

"I have a buggy waiting outside to take him to the museum," Fairchild said, "and another one for you."

"But," she asked, "where am I going?"

"Clint, why don't you go on ahead?" Fairchild said. "We'll see you later."

"Fine with me," Clint said, and left the diningroom. As he went out the front door he thought he heard raised voices.

Chapter Twenty-One

The driver waiting out front was the one who had driven him and Charlotte around the day before, so he had no qualms about getting into the buggy.

"No Miss Goodrich today, sir?" the man asked.

"Afraid not," Clint said. "Just me."

"To the museum?"

"Yes."

"Let's go!" the man yelled at the horse, who almost bolted.

***

When Clint got to the museum he went directly to Jayne Kennedy's office. Since the display case was there, he assumed the tools he had asked for would be there, as well.

As he entered, Jayne looked up from her desk.

"Sorry," he said, "I guess I should've knocked."

"It's okay," she said. "No problem. Are you alone?"

"Yes, Fairchild had something else for Charlotte to do, and when I left the house I think they were fighting."

"That's happening more and more," Jayne said. "I think Charlotte's looking to get fired. She's been very unhappy since Walter gave me this job."

"I get that impression."

"Well, there's nothing I can do about that," Jayne said. "You're probably looking for your tools."

"That's exactly what I'm looking for."

"They're over there by the display case."

Clint walked over, saw a leather bag on the floor near the case. When he looked inside he saw all the tools he thought he'd need.

"Now I need a flat surface to work on," he told Jayne.

"Use that conference table."

"It might get scratched."

"That's all right," she said. "If it does, I'll just have Walter buy me a new one."

"Do you have that much control over him?" Clint asked.

"Hey, if he wants me to stay he has to keep me happy."

"All right, then," Clint said. He took off his jacket and threw it on a chair, then walked to the display case.

"Do you want to take off your gun?" she asked.

"Not particularly," he said, thinking about what had happened at the telegraph office. Who knew when those guys might come back around?

"Can we unlock this?" he asked, standing in front of the display.

"Of course."

She came around from behind her desk and unlocked the case for him.

"Thank you."

"I have some things to do out in the museum," Jayne said. "The room is yours."

"Thanks."

"When I come in later I can bring some coffee."

"Sounds good."

She stared at him for a few moments. When he was about to ask what was on her mind, she closed her eyes, shook her head, and left the office. Whatever she had been thinking, maybe she would share it later.

He stared down at the flintlock and blunderbuss. His intention was to take them apart and inspect them closely, to be sure they were constructed of materials that dated from the early 1700s. He knew from history that Blackbeard carried more than one flintlock. So even if the flintlock wasn't his, the blunderbuss would probably turn out to be Blackbeard's Gun.

"I thought you might need these," Jayne said, reentering. She was carrying some bolts of cloth.

"Thanks, that'll be helpful."

He accepted them and, as she was leaving the room, he spread one bolt over the conference table. Next, he set the flintlock and the blunderbuss side-by-side, deciding which one to dismantle first. The telegram from his friend in New York gave him a few hints of what to look for. His Philadelphia friend, Henry Sandstone, was not only a gunsmith, but an expert on every kind of gun there was. He was excited to see the pieces, evidenced by the fact he said he would be in Ocracoke as fast as he could get there.

But until Sandstone arrived, it was all up to Clint. He spread his tools on the cloth alongside the flintlock and blunderbuss. But when he picked up the blunderbuss he noticed something immediately.

The weight was off.

He hefted it, put it down, picked it up again and did the same. Then he set it down and picked up the flintlock.

Same thing.

Bad weight.

He put the flintlock down and turned as Jayne came back into the room, carrying two cups of coffee.

"What's wrong?" she asked, setting the cups down.

"This flintlock and blunderbuss . . ."

"Yes?"

"They're not the same ones I looked at yesterday."

Chapter Twenty-Two

"What?"

"These aren't the same pieces I looked at yesterday," Clint repeated.

"That can't be."

"Was this room locked last night?"

"Absolutely," she said. "And the building was locked."

"But no security men, right?"

"Not yet," she said. "We haven't had the chance to hire new men, yet."

"And that's why a switch was made," Clint said. "Somebody knew we were going to increase security, so it had to be last night."

"But . . . who?" she asked. "Who could have done it?"

"That's what I'd like to find out," Clint said. "Starting with . . . I thought Fairchild was the only one with a key to this case. Yet, you opened it for me with a key."

"But . . . I'm the curator," she said. "I have to have a key to everything."

"Do you know what that means, Jayne?" Clint asked. "That means that only two people could have made this switch happen. You, or Fairchild."

"What?" she asked. "That's crazy. Why would Walter steal the guns from his own museum?"

"So you're saying it wasn't him?"

"Of course it wasn't him!"

"Then that means it was you," Clint said.

"That's even crazier," she said.

"So then who?"

"I don't know," Jayne Kennedy said, "but I'm sure Walter will expect you to find out."

"Me? Why me?"

"Didn't he hire you for security?"

"He hired me to authenticate the two pieces," Clint said. "Well, if they're gone I can't do that. And he hired me to look over security measures and make some suggestions. I think I've done that. As far as I'm concerned, I can leave town and head back West."

"No, no," she said, "you can't do that. Somebody has to find those guns."

"Don't you have any law, here?"

"We have a sheriff," she said, "but he's not very impressive."

"Still," Clint said, "it's his job. You better send somebody for him."

"I'll send for him," Jayne said, "but I don't think it'll do any good."

"And send for Walter, as well."

"I don't know where he is," she said. "Didn't he tell you?"

"He was going somewhere with Charlotte," Clint said. "You don't suppose . . ."

"Suppose what?"

"Well, does Walter have a woman in his life?"

"Wait," Jayne said. "Are you asking me if Walter and Charlotte are . . . involved? My God, you think they're having sex?"

"Well, if not with her . . ."

"Oh," she said, looking appalled, "now you're asking me if I'm having sex with him?"

"Look, Jayne—"

"No, you look," she said, moving toward the door. She slammed it closed and locked it. Then she turned and, very deliberately, removed every stich of clothing until she was naked.

"He's an old man," she said, again, "do you really think he could handle anything like this?"

She put her hands on her hips and posed for him, one knee slightly bent, her large breasts thrust out at him.

"I—I suppose not," he said.

"And what about you?" She walked across the room, stood right in front of him. "Do you think you can handle this?" She put her hands over her head and twirled around a few times, laughing.

"If you'll stay still," he said, "I guess we'll find out."

He grabbed her, pulled her hot body close to him, and kissed her, not having to lean down at all to do it.

She ran her hands over his body and pressed her mouth to his ear.

"I planned this," she said.

"The switch?"

"The sex."

He knew he should have pushed her away and concentrate on the missing pieces, but she not only filled his hands and arms, but his senses, as well.

She pressed her hand to his crotch, felt the bulge in his pants, and said, "Hmm, I think you're going to be able to handle me very well, if this is any indication."

She started to undo his belt, but he slapped her hands away.

"Before we get to that," he said, "I think I smell that somebody's ready."

He slid his hand down between her legs to probe her wetness.

As he got down on his knees she reached for his head and said, "You bastard."

Chapter Twenty-Three

On his knees Clint pressed his face to the golden patch of hair there. Jayne gasped as his tongue touched her, leaned back against the conference table, taking her weight on both hands, and spread her legs further for him.

Clint ran his hands up and down her thighs and legs as he lapped at her wet pussy avidly with his tongue. When he heard her gasp and felt her legs begin to quiver he took his mouth away and stood up, breathless from his own efforts.

She looked at his face, the lower half of which was glistening with her juices, and then watched as he undressed, first setting his gunbelt aside, but within reach.

When he was naked she stared at his hard, jutting cock as he moved toward her. She reached out and grabbed it with one hand.

"Wait," she said. "There's no room . . ." The table behind her was covered with the cloth, the flintlock and the blunderbuss.

"Here," she said, and tugged him toward her oversized desk.

"But there's—" he said, starting to point out that her desk was covered with work.

She cut him off by sweeping her arms across the surface, clearing the top by dumping everything onto the floor.

As they climbed on the desk together, he wondered if she had done this before. She didn't seem to be worried that their combined weight might collapse it.

She was a strong girl, and she was trying to get on top, but he managed to flip her over and attain a dominant position. He pinned her hands above her head, moved his hips and pierced her with his cock. She was so wet he slid in to the hilt very easily.

Once he was inside, there was no reason to pin her hands any more. He released her, and she quickly put her arms around him and began raking his back with her nails. Luckily, they were short. Whatever damage they caused would be minimal, and whatever pain they were causing was almost pleasurable, under the circumstances.

He slid his hands down around to her butt, gripped it and, with every lunge of his hips, pulled her to him. The penetration was so deep, so complete, that she grunted with every thrust. The desk held, but it hopped noisily a few inches each time. However, they were both so involved with each other that neither of them was concerned about the noise being heard outside the door.

He could tell that she still wanted to exert her strength and get on top, but a struggle could have caused them both to fall off the desk. One of them had to give in, and it wasn't going to be her, so he finally relented and let her change places.

They did so without severing their connection, and once she was on top he saw the benefit of it. As she started to ride him he was afforded a wonderful view of her large, heaving breasts, large pink nipples, and the expression of pure lust and delight on her beautiful face.

He reached for her, then, gripping her breasts and thumbing her nipples as she continued to bounce on him harder and harder, mindlessly seeking her own gratification. So, in the end, he closed his eyes and gave in to his own lust. They continued to fill the room with the sound of slapping wet flesh until she muffled a scream and he did the same with a mighty groan of both pleasure and pain . . .

**

"We better hurry and get dressed," she said, sliding off the desk.

"This doesn't change anything, Jayne," he said, as they did so.

"I know," she said, "but we had to get this out of the way, didn't we? I mean, you did sleep with Charlotte already, didn't you?"

"What does that matter?"

She smiled.

"It matters that she got to you first," she said. "But I bet you're too much of a gentleman to say who was the best, huh?"

He remained silent as he strapped on his gun.

"I thought so."

She walked to the door and unlocked it. She peered outside. If anyone had been out there listening, they were long gone.

"I think we got away with it." She turned her back to the door, facing him, and leaned against it, looking pleased with herself. "You don't wonder any longer if I'm having sex with Walter, do you?"

"No," he said, "you were right, he couldn't handle it. But you might want to go and get somebody to fetch the sheriff, now."

"Right, right," she said. "That's what I was going to do before you interrupted me."

As she went out the door he yelled out, "I interrupted you?"

Chapter Twenty-Four

Before the sheriff arrived, Walter Fairchild came walking in.

"So?" he asked. "Any good news?"

Clint told him.

"That's impossible!" He glared at Jayne.

"I can't tell," she said. "According to Clint, that's what's happened."

Fairchild looked at Clint.

"Are you telling me the truth?"

"Whoa," Clint said. "I was doing the job you told me to do. Are you thinking I walked off with the real guns?"

"You couldn't get in here to do that," Fairchild said. "We have the only keys."

"That's right," Clint said.

"But you could be telling us a lie," the older man went on, "that these pieces aren't real. We only have your word for that."

"And my word is what you hired me for," Clint reminded him.

"Yes, yes," Fairchild said, "all right, "I'm . . . I'm clutching at straws, here. If none of the three of us did this, then who did? And how?"

"That's up to your local law to find out," Clint said. "We've sent for him."

"Sheriff Lundigan? The man's a useless ass!"

"Well," Clint said, "he's what you've got."

"Show me," Fairchild said.

"Where's Charlotte?" Jayne asked.

"Running an errand," her boss said, as he walked to the table with Clint.

Fairchild looked down at the two pieces and said, "How can you tell? They looked the same to me."

"Weight," Clint said. "At least, to start with." He picked up the blunderbuss. "This one's heavier."

Fairchild took it.

"Feels the same to me."

"It would." Clint took it back, set it down, handed the man the flintlock.

"Same with this one."

"Right," Clint said, taking it back. "Nobody would notice except someone who handles guns."

"Still . . . if they look like the real thing . . ."

"I've got another expert coming down to have a look," Clint said.

"What? I didn't okay that. Who's paying him?"

"He's doing it as a favor to me," Clint said. "He works for the Philadelphia Police Department."

"And he'll be able to tell if these are real?"

"He will."

"And then, when we get the other ones back . . ."

"Those, too."

"And what if you and he are cooking something up—"

"Don't start that again," Clint said.

"All right, all right," Fairchild said. "I suppose the three of us are just going to have to trust each other."

"And what about Charlotte?" Jayne asked. She was seated at her desk, where everything that had been strewn about the floor was now back in place—more or less.

"What about her?" Fairchild asked.

"Couldn't she have something to do with it?"

"Well," Fairchild said, "she doesn't have a key."

"She could've told somebody about the pieces," Jayne said. "And they came and stole them."

"But they didn't steal them," the man said, "they replaced them with duplicates. Now that would have taken planning."

"Does she have a boyfriend?" Clint asked.

"Not Charlotte," Fairchild said. "She's all about her work."

Clint knew that wasn't true, but kept his mouth shut.

"Where's that damn sheriff?" he said.

Just then there was a knock on the door and Jayne called, "Come in."

A well-dressed man wearing a badge on the vest of his three piece suit entered.

"I understand you folks had a theft here?" he asked.

"Come on in, Sheriff," Jayne said.

The man entered and said, "Miss Kennedy, as lovely as ever."

The sheriff was a tall, attractive man in his 30s, and Clint suddenly wondered if he'd ever been in the office before, maybe on the desk?

Jayne came around and shook his hand.

"Mr. Fairchild," the sheriff said, shaking hands again. "First time I've been in your fine establishment. Quite impressive."

"Thank you. Sheriff Lundigan, this is Clint Adams. I've retained his services."

Sheriff Lundigan stared at Clint for a moment, then put his hand out warily to shake.

"Is that Clint Adams, the Gunsmith?" he asked.

"The same," Fairchild said.

"What could you be needing a gunfighter for, Mr. Fairchild?" the sheriff asked. "I mean, around here."

"His expertise, Sheriff," Fairchild replied.

He went on to tell Lundigan about the two pieces that had been found in the cave, how Clint had been hired to authenticate them, and how before that could happen. They had been switched.

"Switched?" the lawman asked. "How could that happen? And why?"

"The why is simple," Clint said, speaking for the first time since the lawman had arrived. "Money. They'd be pretty valuable to a collector."

"Okay, then who?" Lundigan asked.

"That's the question," Fairchild said, "that we've brought you here to answer."

"Me?" the lawman asked.

"Well, that's your job, isn't it?" Jayne asked.

"I keep the peace," the sheriff said, "but I'm not a detective. If we knew who it was I could go and find them, arrest them. But finding out who did it, that's work for a detective." He looked at Fairchild. "Maybe you need somebody like a Pinkerton."

"Sheriff," Fairchild said, "too many people already know about these pieces. I'm not bringing the Pinkertons in."

"Well . . . I'll do what I can, then. Ask around."

"Discreetly, please," Fairchild said.

"What other way?" Lundigan asked, and left the room.

Chapter Twenty-Five

"See what I mean?" Fairchild said. "Useless."

"Well," Clint said, "he'll do whatever he can."

"That's not enough!" Fairchild exclaimed. "We need you."

"Look, I've told you what to do to beef up your security," Clint said. "And I've examined these two pieces and told you they're not real. I can't do anything else until the real pieces turn up."

"But what if they never do?" Jayne asked.

"That's not my problem," Clint said.

Fairchild and Jayne looked at each other, as if communicating without words.

"Unless . . ." Clint said.

"Unless what?" Fairchild asked.

"Since I got here I've had the feeling that something's going on," Clint said. "Something you're not letting me in on. I think you're both—and maybe Charlotte, as well—keeping something from me."

Fairchild and Jayne exchanged that look, once again.

"If you want my help," Clint said, "you're going to have to tell me everything."

"I think he's right, Walter," Jayne said. "We can't keep anything from him. We have to tell him everything."

"All right," Fairchild said, "but not here. At the house, tonight. I'll ask you if you could please work on security for tonight."

"I've got some men coming in for an interview," Jayne told him.

"Were you going to tell me that?"

"Yes," Jayne said, "yes, I would've told you after you worked on the pieces for a while."

"All right," Clint said, "I'll pick some men and we'll put them on day and night shifts—although I don't see the point, now."

"We'll discuss it all tonight," Fairchild said. "Jayne, you'll come to supper."

"Yes, sir."

"And let Clint use your office to interview the men."

"Of course."

"I'll see you both tonight," Fairchild said. "Seven sharp."

He turned and left the office.

"You know what's going on, don't you?" Clint asked her. "You could tell me now."

"And get myself fired," she said. "I'm sorry, but you'll have to wait. I'll go and see if the security applicants are here."

While she was gone Clint took the time to put the fake guns back in the display case, locking it with the key Jayne had left behind.

He went over to her desk, but decided not to interview them across the surface where he and Jayne had just had sex. Instead, he went to the now bare conference table and sat there, waiting.

Jayne came in leading 6 men. Clint thought that didn't leave him a big choice, taking 3 of the 6.

Jayne looked at the desk, seemed confused, then saw Clint seated at the conference table.

"I'd like to take them one-by-one," he told her.

"Certainly," she said, pointing. "You first, the rest can wait outside."

Clint started his first interview . . .

***

He spent the afternoon interviewing the 6 men. He found 2 he actually liked, and then chose one from the final 4—the best of a bad lot.

When Jayne came back in he said, "These are our three new security guards. Let's put them together with Coates and they can work out who does days and who does nights."

"Whatever you say," Jayne said. "Will you be here when I get back?"

"No, I'm going to the house. I'll see you at supper, tonight."

"Oh. Well," She said, seeming disappointed, "All right."

She took the men to meet Coates, and Clint went out the front door, discovered that Fairchild had left the buggy and driver waiting for him.

"You been here all day?" he asked the same driver he'd had that morning.

"Pretty much."

"Take me back to the house and then I think you can have the rest of the night off."

"That suits me."

***

When he entered the house it felt empty. He didn't see any staff, or Fairchild, even when he looked in the man's library. And there was no sign of Charlotte. He wondered what she had been doing all day?

He decided to go upstairs and use the indoor plumbing to draw himself a nice bath. He planned to soak in it, with his gunbelt close by.

Chapter Twenty-Six

When Clint came down for supper Walter Fairchild was seated at the diningroom table, a glass of red wine in front of him. Also seated was Jayne Kennedy, wearing a beautiful low-cut dress that showed off the swollen slopes of her breasts. She had a glass of white wine on the table in front of her.

Also in the room, but not seated, was Charlotte. She was standing off to one side, wearing a shoulder baring dress, her arms folded firmly across her breasts. Clint had the feeling he had interrupted a heated discussion, as her face was very red, and her body was taut with tension.

"Sorry I'm late," he said.

"You're not," Fairchild assured him. "We were all a bit early. Charlotte, why don't you tell cook she can serve the food now."

Charlotte glared at him, and Jayne pushed her chair back, saying, "Oh, I'll do it."

"Have a seat, Clint," Fairchild said. "I've arranged to have some beer for you, tonight."

"I appreciate that," Clint said, "but what I'd like instead of beer are some answers."

Jayne came back from the kitchen carrying a mug of beer, which she handed to Clint. Then she turned to Fairchild and said, "She's bringing supper right in."

She sat back down, across from her host and employer.

Clint saw a glass of white wine the table, assumed it was Charlotte's, picked it up and carried it over to her.

She took it from him and whispered, "They're still going to lie to you."

"We'll talk after," he said, then raised his voice. "You're welcome. Why don't we sit?"

He escorted her to her place at the table, held her chair for her, then walked around and sat across from her.

"There," Fairchild said, "we're all here."

The cook came out of the kitchen and started serving the food, going back in several more times before she was done. The table was covered with chicken, vegetables, and a tureen of soup.

"You can go back to the kitchen, Cook," Fairchild said, "we'll serve ourselves."

"Yes, sir," she said, and withdrew.

"Please," Fairchild told his guests, "help yourselves to soup. Ladies first."

Jayne went first, then Clint passed the tureen to Charlotte. When they all had soup they ate, and talked.

"Did you get the security taken care of?" Fairchild asked Jayne.

"Yes," she said. "Your man Coates took charge, and set the watches."

"Which did he take for himself?"

"Night."

"That's good. And the pieces are locked up?"

"You mean, the phony pieces?"

"Yes," Clint said, "they should be locked away as if they were real. You haven't told anyone, have you?"

"Of course not!" Fairchild said. "That's the last thing we want anyone to know."

"Then," Clint said, "if the word gets around we'll know it came from the sheriff."

"Yes, I wish you had consulted me before sending for him," Fairchild said.

"That's water under the bridge," Clint said. "Why don't you start telling me what I don't know?"

"Let's attack this chicken while it's still hot," Fairchild suggested. "We can get to that, later."

Clint looked at Charlotte, who lifted her chin. He knew that, of the three, he just might have her on his side.

***

They demolished the food on the table, leaving nothing but empty vegetable plates and chicken bones.

"Let's go to the livingroom," Fairchild said, sliding his chair back. "Cook will bring more drinks."

They all rose and walked to the livingroom. Moments later the cook appeared carrying a tray of drinks—three glasses of wine and a mug of cold beer.

"Thank you," Clint said, when she held the tray out to him.

After they all had their drinks, she turned and left.

"All right, Walter," Clint said, "I'm ready."

"First, let me explain my position," Fairchild said. "I am a lone voice on the board. The other five members normally band against me."

"But . . ."

"But I have more money than the five of them put together," Fairchild went on.

"And that makes you even?"

"It puts me slightly ahead," Fairchild said.

"And you have these two by your side," Clint said, indicating Jayne and Charlotte.

"Yes I do."

"Then" Clint said, "I'd think that would put you more than slightly ahead."

Chapter Twenty-Seven

"The Blackbeard pieces were found in the caves," Fairchild said. "That much is true."

"But?"

"But they weren't actually found by us," Fairchild said.

"And by 'us', you mean?"

"People from the museum."

Clint looked at Jayne and Charlotte drinking wine.

"So they were brought to the museum by the people who found them?"

Fairchild hesitated, then said, "Not exactly."

"What's 'not exactly' mean?"

Fairchild looked at Charlotte and Jayne—for support, Clint assumed.

"The first time they were brought to us we turned them away," he said, finally.

"Why?"

"We, uh, told the people who found them that they weren't genuine."

"Even though you thought they could be?"

"Yes."

"Why?"

Fairchild took a sip of his wine.

"Oh, for Chrissake, Walter!" Jayne said. "Because he knew they'd come back again and we'd be able to get them cheaper, which we did."

"And then?"

"And then they found out that we thought they were real, and were having them authenticated," Jayne said. "They came back for more money, but Walter wouldn't give it to them. So they said they were going to take them back."

"That's when I put the two security men in place," Fairchild said.

"And only two," Clint reminded him. "And only during the day."

"Duly noted," Fairchild said.

"So you cheated them," Clint said.

"Not cheated," Fairchild said.

"We prefer to say we made a heady bargain," Jayne said.

"Okay," Clint said, "so do we think these other people stole the pieces back? Or rather, replaced them with fakes?"

"No," Fairchild said. "They couldn't have built fakes that good that fast."

"And they're not smart enough to have done it," Jayne said.

Clint looked at Charlotte.

"Don't look at me," she said. "I never met them."

Clint looked at Fairchild again. He, Jayne and Charlotte were still standing apart.

"Who are they?"

"Locals," Fairchild said. "They spend their time on the beaches, looking for treasure."

"And they found some."

"Yes."

"Only you cheated them out of it."

Fairchild looked pained.

"Not cheated—"

"Okay, forget that," Clint said. "Do you know where they live?"

"No," Fairchild said. "Only their last name."

"Which is?"

"Teach."

"Okay, so—wait. Teach?"

Fairchild nodded.

"Isn't that—"

"Yes," Fairchild said. "Blackbeard's real name. Edward Teach."

"So…"So they claim to be descendants of Blackbeard the Pirate."

Chapter Twenty-Eight

"And are they?" Clint asked.

"Who knows?" Fairchild asked. "They've been here longer than I have. The people in town know them, think they're all crazy."

"All?"

"It's a family," Fairchild said. "Three brothers, one sister . . ."

". . . and an old Aunt who's the head of the family."

They all turned and looked at Charlotte.

"I was born here, remember?" she said. "I even went to school with some of them."

"Why didn't you tell us that when we were dealing with them?" Fairchild asked.

"You never asked me," Charlotte said. "You and Jayne were busy dealing with them yourselves."

"Yes, well," Fairchild said, "that may have been an error. What else do you know?"

"Are they descendants of Teach?" Clint asked.

"That I don't know for sure," Charlotte said. "All I know is what I've heard all my life, that the Teach family is descended from Blackbeard."

Clint looked at Fairchild.

"It's doubtful," the man said.

"But possible?" Clint asked.

"Well . . . anything's possible."

"So if they are descended from him, the guns belong to them."

"They sold them to us," Fairchild said.

"After you convinced them they weren't authentic."

"Hey," Fairchild said, "they could have had them authenticated before they came to us."

"They're simple people," Charlotte said. "They wouldn't have had any idea how to do that."

"Don't make excuses for them, Charlotte," Fairchild said.

"I'm just telling you what I know."

"Keep doing that, Charlotte," Clint said. "I need it."

"What are you going to do?" Fairchild asked.

"I'm going to find the real pieces," Clint said. "Not because you want me to, or you're paying me to, but because I want to."

"So what's your first step?"

"I want to talk with the Teach family," Clint said. He looked at Charlotte. "Can you arrange a meeting?"

"Yes."

"How do you know that?" Jayne asked.

"Because they came to me in the first place, remember?" Charlotte asked. "I went to school with Tara, the sister, who came to me. Now I can go to her."

"Will they trust you?" Clint asked. "After what happened? He looked at Fairchild, but still spoke to Charlotte. "After Walter cheated them?"

"I didn't cheat—" Fairchild started, but stopped himself short.

"I think they will," Charlotte said. "I think they know I didn't go along with it."

"Good," Clint said. "Then set a meeting."

"I will."

"In fact," Clint said, "take me with you."

"That might not be smart," she said. "If we approach their house—"

"It'll be quicker," Clint said. "I'm hoping those real pieces are still close by."

"All right," she said. "We can go to their place tomorrow morning."

"Good," Clint said. To Fairchild he said, "What else do you have to tell me?"

"About what?"

"Whatever you've been keeping from me."

Fairchild shook his head.

"That's it."

"You just didn't want me to know that you cheated to get the pieces?"

"I didn't cheat—" Fairchild stopped again.

"It wasn't exactly on the up-and-up, admittedly," Jayne said. "I don't think Walter wanted you to know that."

Walter Fairchild sipped his wine, looking extremely uncomfortable.

"He did what he thought was right for the museum, Clint," Jayne said.

"I get that, Jayne," Clint said. He set his mug down. "I think I'm going to retire to my room." He turned to Charlotte. "Early tomorrow morning?"

"Eight?"

"That's good."

"I'll be out front."

Clint nodded. He walked to the doorway, then turned.

"Now I'll leave you to fight among yourselves," he said. "Just try to keep it down to a low roar."

He left the room and headed up the stairs to his bedroom.

Chapter Twenty-Nine

The knock on his door a couple of hours later was light. He felt it was either Charlotte or Jayne. Fairchild wouldn't have that light a touch.

He opened it a crack, saw it was Jayne, then opened it wide. She looked at the gun in his hand.

"My, but you are a careful man," Jayne said.

"And therefore," he said, "I'm still alive. What can I do for you?"

"Can I come in?"

"What do you have in mind?"

"Not that," she said. "Not in Walter's house, anyway. I just want to talk."

"Come ahead, then."

He walked to the bedpost and holstered the gun while she closed the door.

"I don't have anything to offer you," he said. "Not even water."

"That's all right," she said. "I just wanted to clear something up."

She was still wearing the same dress she had worn to supper. Clint had removed his boots and unbuttoned his shirt. There was one chair in the room and she took it. He sat on the bed.

"What's on your mind?" he asked.

"It's Walter," she said. "I don't think he's telling any of us the truth."

"So other than you and he keeping things from me, you think he's keeping things from you?"

"Yes," she said, "from me and Charlotte."

"And what about you and Charlotte?"

"Yes, well, we're never very open with each other," she admitted.

Jayne had been there five minutes and already the room was filled with the scent of her—both her perfume, and her natural fragrance.

"Is that what you wanted to tell me?"

"Yes, don't trust Walter," she said, "and just to be on the safe side, don't trust Charlotte. They seem to be having definite problems with each other."

"And you?"

"I have problems with Charlotte, but Walter and I seem to get along, even if he is keeping some things from me."

"No," Clint said, "I mean, should I trust you?"

She sat with her knees together, and her hands on her knees.

"Probably not," she answered, looking down. "But I'm hoping you will."

"I guess we'll just have to wait and see," Clint said. "Let's get some sleep."

"Yes," she said, standing. "I'll be in a room down the hall . . . if you need me."

"You're staying here?"

"Walter suggested it." She went to the door, opened it, then looked at him again. Maybe she was hoping he would ask her to stay. "Good night, Clint."

"Good night, Jayne."

***

The next knock came only ten minutes later. He hadn't even had time to get back into the Dickens he was reading.

"Well, either shoot me or let me in," Charlotte said.

"Come on in."

He stowed his gun away and turned to her.

"I saw her," she said. "Jayne. She was in your room."

"Charlotte—"

"But not long enough to do anything but talk," Charlotte went on. "What did she want?"

"She wants me to trust her."

"Ha! Not likely, right?" Charlotte was also still in the dress she had worn to supper.

"Walter asked you to stay the night?" Clint asked.

"Yes, he said you and I could leave from here in the morning. Clint, you can't trust either one of them."

"I'm finding that out," he said.

"But you can trust me."

"Can I?"

"You know you can!"

"Well," he said, "tomorrow will go a long way towards proving that."

"I'm not like Jayne, Clint," Charlotte said. "You know that."

"I do know that, Charlotte."

"Charlie," she said.

"What?"

"You can call me Charlie," she said. "Nobody's called me that in . . . in a long time."

He thought about taking her into his arms, but he knew what that would lead to. He didn't want to dally with either woman in Fairchild's house.

"Okay, Charlie," he said. "I think we ought to get some sleep."

"Yes, of course," she said. "I'm at the other end of the hall, if you need me."

"All right. Good night, Charlie."

"Good night, Clint."

She eased out of the room and closed the door gently.

***

Clint half expected another knock at his door, but who would it be this time? Fairchild himself? Or one of the women, deciding to come back to try to get into his bed.

He decided if there was another light knocking, that he would pretend to be asleep. He was through talking for the night.

Tomorrow he would do more than talk.

***

When the knock came Walter Fairchild put on his robe and opened the door.

"What are you doing here?" he asked, as Jayne entered, also wearing a robe. "I thought you were going to be with Clint." He closed the door.

She turned to face him.

"So did I," she said. "He sent me away."

"Really?" Fairchild said. "He's got more will power than I thought."

Jayne opened her robe and let it fall to the floor. Beneath it, she was completely naked.

"More than you have?" she asked.

Chapter Thirty

In the morning Clint found Charlotte waiting for him in the diningroom rather than outside.

"Breakfast?" she asked. "Before we head out?"

"Just you and me?"

"Looks like it."

He shrugged.

"Fine."

They sat across from each other, and the cook brought out their breakfast—bacon-and-eggs, and biscuits, washed down with coffee.

"Where are we heading?" he asked. "Into town?"

"No," she said, "the Teach family has some homes outside of town."

"Homes?"

"The children are grown," she said. "They have their own homes."

"I should have thought of that," Clint said, as they ate. "You said they went to school with you."

"Yes," Charlotte said, "Tara did, and one of her brothers, Mickey."

"Are they who we're going to see?"

"Tara will talk to me," she said. "Mickey won't."

"And the others?"

"The older brother's name is Lenny. He's the one who came to me about the pieces. I took him to Fairchild."

"And were you part of the negotiations?"

"No," she said. "After I put them together, Fairchild . . . dismissed me."

"He didn't want you to know what he was doing."

"What he and Jayne were doing," Charlotte said, lowering her voice. "Don't forget, they're a pair."

"I'm not forgetting anything," he told her, and they continued eating.

***

After breakfast they went out front and found the driver and buggy waiting for them. It was the same driver he'd had before.

"What's your name?" Clint asked.

"Frank."

"Okay, Frank, I guess you know Miss Goodrich."

"I do, Sir. Good morning, Miss. Where to, today?"

"Miss Goodrich will give you directions," Clint said. "We're going to visit the descendants of Blackbeard the Pirate."

"Really?"

"So they claim."

"Oh," Frank said, "the Teaches."

"Do you know where they live?"

"I heard about them, but I don't know where they live."

"Okay, then," Clint said, helping Charlotte into the buggy and then joining her. "Like I said, Miss Goodrich knows the way."

"Head toward town, Frank," she said. "And then take the beach road when we get to it."

"Yes, Miss."

He shook the reins and they headed off.

***

Several miles outside of town they came to the road Charlotte had called the beach road. As far as Clint could see, though, it wasn't marked.

"Does this road have a name?" he asked, as Frank turned onto it.

"Not specifically," Charlotte said, "but the locals do call it Beach Road."

"Do they get their mail?"

"No, they go to town to the post office to pick it up," Charlotte said. "Usually, one family member goes in and gets it for all of them."

Clint had recently spent some time in Kentucky and West Virginia, involved with the Hatfield and McCoy families. The Teach family was starting to remind him of that clan.

***

After a couple of miles Charlotte leaned forward and tapped Frank on the shoulder.

"That's far enough, Frank."

"I don't see any houses," Clint said.

"They'll be further down," she told him. "We should walk from here. If they hear a buggy coming, somebody might take a shot."

Yep, Clint thought, more and more like the Hatfields and McCoys.

He helped her down. "Go ahead, lead the way."

"I should go alone, first, Clint," she said.

"That doesn't sound very safe to me."

"They won't take a shot at me."

"Whose house are you going to first?"

"Tara's."

"Does she live alone?"

"Yes," Charlotte said, "she's a young widow."

"All right," Clint said, "I'll let you go alone, but at the first sign of trouble, Charlie, I'm going to come running."

Charlotte stood on her toes, kissed him, stroked his face and said, "I wouldn't have it any other way."

Chapter Thirty-One

Clint had said he would let her go in alone, but he didn't say anything about not following her.

He gave her a bit of a head start, then started off after her. Her boots had distinctive heels that were leaving an easy trail to follow.

He could smell the salt water off in the distance, and even hear the tide breaking. The Teach family may not have lived on the beach, but they lived damn close to it.

Finally, Clint came around a curve and stopped when he saw a house. Charlotte was on the porch, about to knock on the door, so he ducked down and watched . . .

***

When Charlotte got to the door she realized it had been a lot of years since she had last been there. Bringing Lenny to see Walter Fairchild had not involved Tara much, at all, so this would actually be the first time she spoke to her in years.

She knocked on the door and waited. When it opened, Tara stared out at her. She hadn't changed much, still a pretty, long-haired redhead.

"Tara?"

"Charlie?" Tara frowned at her. "What the hell are ya doin' here?"

"I came to see you."

"I kin see that. But why?"

"Can I come in?"

Tara thought a minute, then stepped out and said, "No," closing the door firmly behind her. "We can talk out here on the porch."

"All right," Charlotte said. "There's been a problem at the museum."

"And after the way they cheated my family, why should I care about that?"

"Because your brothers might be in trouble," Charlotte said. "The law is involved."

"What's that idiot sheriff accusin' my brothers of doin', now?" Tara asked.

"Those guns the museum brought from Lenny? They've been stolen."

Tara stared at her for a few moments, then started laughing.

"That's rich. The guns your boss stole from my family got stolen?" She started to laugh, again, so loud Clint could hear her from his vantage point.

"Tara!"

The girl stopped laughing.

"This is serious. I need to talk to Lenny."

"Why?" Tara asked. "You think my brother stole them?"

"They weren't stolen, exactly," Charlotte said. "They were . . . replaced."

"Replaced?"

"With phonies."

"So your boss tells my brother that the guns are phony, and then he ends up with phonies?" Tara laughed again. "This keeps gettin' better and better. What else you got?"

"Do you know who Clint Adams is?"

Tara became serious.

"He's the Gunsmith," Tara said. "What's he got to do with any of this?"

"He's who my boss hired to get the real guns back," Charlotte said.

"Hmm," Tara said. "Interesting."

"Will you take us to Lenny?"

"No," Tara said. "Your Gunsmith is gonna have to talk to me first."

"I can arrange that."

"When?"

"Well . . . right now. I just have to go back up the road and get him."

"Good," Tara said. "I'll go inside and . . . wait. When you bring him back, send him in." She went to the door, then turned. "And you stay out here."

Charlotte waited for the door to slam, then turned and went back down the steps.

***

Clint watched the two women talk on the porch, and then Tara Teach—or Tara Williams, since she kept her dead husband's last name—went back into her house and Charlotte started walking back.

He stepped out.

"Whoa!" She reared back, momentarily startled. "What are you doing here?"

"Keeping an eye on you," he said. "What happened? She wouldn't agree to help?"

"She will," Charlotte said, "after she talks to you."

"I thought you said the Teach family wouldn't talk to anybody but you."

"I did say that but once I told her you were involved, she wanted to talk to you."

"When?"

"Now," Charlotte said getting behind him and pushing him toward the house, "right now!"

Chapter Thirty-Two

Charlotte took Clint to the front door of Tara Williams' house.

"Go on in," she said. "She's waitin'?"

"Shouldn't we knock?"

"No," Charlotte said, "Just go in."

Clint opened the door and entered.

On the outside the house looked almost abandoned, with boards missing from the porch and the walls, shingles hanging askew. The inside, however, had been given much more care, and by a woman. He saw a well-kept kitchen, a sitting area—not large enough to be a living-room—with a sofa and chair. And through another doorway he could see a bed, and some shadows moving.

"Hello," he called.

"I'll be right out," a girl's voice called from the bedroom.

Moments later the shadows in the bedroom became a person, and a pretty girl with red hair and freckles stepped out.

"Are you Clint Adams?" she asked.

"That's right. And you're Tara?"

When he had seen her on the porch she had been wearing jeans and an old shirt. Now she was wearing a pretty blue dress that looked like something she would wear to a barn dance.

"You wanna drink?" she asked. "All I got is some moonshine my brothers made."

"No, that's okay," Clint said. "Charlotte told you that I want to talk to your brother? The one who first found the guns?"

"Yeah, Lenny," Tara said. "He's my oldest brother."

"Do you think he'd talk to me?"

She put her hands behind her back and swiveled from side-to-side.

"He might, if I asked him to."

"And how would I get you to do that?" he asked. "Pay you?"

"I don't need your money."

"Then what?"

"I been a widow for about five years," she said. "You know what that means in my family?"

"What?"

"I ain't had a man's hands on me in all that time."

"Why not?"

"My brothers," she said. "Men around here are afraid of them. You know why?"

"Because they're descended from Blackbeard the Pirate?"

"Heck no," she said. "That's just somethin' we tell people on account we got the same last name."

"So it's not true?"

"Who knows?" she asked. "Could be. But that don't matter."

Clint thought he knew what she was going to ask, and wondered if Charlotte knew, as well?

"Tara—"

"You got a reputation with guns and women," she pointed out. "That means you kin gimme what I want, and you ain't afraid of my brothers."

"Tara—" he tried again, but she wasn't listening.

Apparently, she had put the dress on because it would be easy to take off, which was what she did, showing him that she was a natural redhead. The patch of hair between her thighs was liked burnished copper, and her small breasts were covered with freckles, and dark nipples.

"You think I'm pretty?" she asked.

"You're real pretty, Tara."

"And," she said, sliding her hand down between her thighs, "I'm already wet for you."

She stepped close to him and held her two wet fingers under his nose.

"See?"

The scent coming off her fingers was a heady one, and he reacted to it.

"Do you live here alone?" he asked

"I do," she said. "It's where I lived with my husband, and after he died I stayed. Don't worry, ain't nobody gonna walk in on us."

He put his arms around her naked body thinking, I hope not.

Chapter Thirty-Three

She was slender and light as he lifted her and carried her into the bedroom. Along the way she started kissing his face, neck, and lips.

He set her down on a bed he wasn't sure would hold the two of them. But since she had lived there with her husband, it must have seen some action, and was still standing.

Since she was definitely already wet and he had the scent in his nostrils, he didn't even bother undressing. He got down on his knees and pressed his face into that copper forest of hair. With his tongue he found the wet lips of her pussy and licked them, before probing further.

"Ooooh, Jesus," she gasped, and reached down to hold his head in her hands. "Even my husband never did that to me!"

Instinctively, she lifted her legs up and spread them for him, holding her ankles in her own hands. He went deep with his tongue, then moved up until he found her rigid clitoris, and settled there for a while.

"Oh Lord," she said, pressing her crotch tight against his face. "Is this that French stuff I been hearin' about?"

He took his face away from her crotch and looked up at her, his face gleaming with her nectar.

"This is what a man does to a woman when he wants to please her," he said. "It doesn't matter what country you're in."

"Well, then, keep doin' it!" she said, grabbing his head and once again pressing his face to her.

But Clint knew that Charlotte was waiting outside. How long would it take for her to decide to barge in?

"No," he said, pulling away from her, "I've got something else for you."

He undressed quickly, and her eyes widened when she saw his engorged cock. Clint could help but be even more excited by the possibility of Charlotte walking in.

He got on the bed with Tara, spread her legs with his knees, and pierced her easily to the core.

"Ohhhhhhh," she groaned, bringing her legs up to wrap about his waist.

He started taking her in long, slow strokes, which she obviously wasn't used to.

"You go so slow," she said. "The men I been with— my Jimmy included—they just got in, fucked me hard, and got out. Then went to sleep."

"Well," he told her, "nobody here is going to do any sleeping . . ."

Before finishing he decided to give her something else she probably never got from the men in her life.

Abruptly, he flipped over, without breaking their connection, and suddenly she was on top.

"Oh!" she said, surprised. "All the men I've known think this makes them weak."

"All I'm thinking about," Clint said, "is making you happy."

That delighted her. Laughing, she started to bounce up and down on him. She enjoyed it so much she couldn't slow down or stop. Her inside sucked the seed right out of Clint, even though he was trying to hold back. And the next second she was grinding herself down on him, trying not to scream from the—pleasure she was feeling.

***

"Do you think she heard?" Tara asked, as they got dressed.

"Who?"

"Charlie," Tara said. "Ain't she out on the porch, waitin'?"

"I, uh, guess she is, but I don't think she heard a thing."

"Would it matter if she did?" she asked. "Is she your woman?"

"No, she's not my woman—"

"But you made her happy the way you just made me happy?" she asked, buttoning her shirt. She had tossed the dress aside. It had served its purpose.

"I hope so."

She put her hands on her hips and said, "I know so!"

He strapped on his gunbelt, which he had kept right by the bed.

"Now will you take me to see your brother?"

"Tell me the truth," she said. "Are you gonna shoot 'im?"

"Why would I shoot him?" he asked. "That's not my intention, at all."

"Well," she said, "if I take you to see him my other brothers might be there, too. Zack and Witt, they like usin' their guns."

"I'll do my best not to shoot anybody," he told her. "I promise."

"Hey," she said, "it don't make no never mind to me if you shoot any of 'em, but it would upset my aunt, and I dearly love her."

"Like I said," he told her, "I'll do my best."

She giggled.

"Seems to me your best is pretty damned good. And if you're as good with a gun as you are with that tallywacker of yours, my brothers would be in lots of trouble if they go for their guns."

Chapter Thirty-Four

They went to the front door and stepped out onto the porch.

Charlotte was there, as he had left her, but she wasn't alone.

"Hello, Adams."

Tara spoke first.

"Pete Anderson," she snapped, "what the hell are you doin' here?"

"Shut your mouth, Tara Teach," the burly Anderson said. "This is between me and Adams."

"My name is Williams," she hissed, but Anderson ignored her.

Anderson had the two men with him that had been in the telegraph office. One of them was standing behind Charlotte with his arm across her chest. Of the two other men, Clint actually recognized one, who had called himself Calendar when he tried to pick him up at the station.

"Are you okay, Charlie?" he asked.

"I'm fine," she said. "They just . . . surprised me."

Clint looked at Anderson.

"What do you want?"

Anderson was seated on the wooden railing, which didn't look strong enough to hold him. Three of the men were standing off the porch, on the ground in front, while the other one—holding Charlotte—was on it.

They all had guns in plain view, this time. No jackets.

Tara was standing next to Clint. He reached out with his left hand and pushed her away.

"I'll ask you again, Anderson," he said. "What do you want?"

"Blackbeard's guns," the man said. "You have them."

"No, I don't," Clint said. "They're in the museum."

"Those are phony," Anderson said. "You have the real ones, somewhere. I want 'em."

Clint didn't know if the man was guessing, or he knew. If he knew that for a fact, then somebody was talking. He hoped it was the sheriff. He didn't like the alternative.

"I don't know where you're getting your information," Clint replied, "but you're wrong."

"Pete," Tara said, "if you hurt me, my brothers ain't gonna like it."

"We ain't here to hurt you, Tara," Anderson said. "Just stay out of the way."

"That's good advice, Tara," Clint said. Then he spoke to Anderson. "Why don't you let Charlie step off to the side, too. Like you said, this is between us."

"Yeah," Anderson said, "you and the five of us." He laughed, looked at the man who was holding Charlotte. "Looks like Bennett likes holdin' your girlfriend, Adams. He might get mad if I make him let her go."

Clint pinned Bennett with a hard stare, but still spoke to Anderson.

"He might get dead if he doesn't."

Bennett looked at Clint, then looked away and swallowed. But he tightened his hold on Charlotte.

"Before this goes any further," Clint said, "who are you working for, Anderson?"

"What makes you think I'm workin' for anybody?" Anderson asked. "Why can't I be workin' for myself?"

"That's not possible," Clint said.

"Why not?"

"You're not smart enough."

Anderson's face grew red, but he didn't go for his gun. Clint knew he had one advantage. They didn't want to kill him until he told them where the guns were.

He, on the other hand, had no compunction about killing them all.

Now!

He drew and fired at Bennett first. The bullet passed very close to Charlotte's head before it struck Bennett in the neck. That was his penance for being so much taller than she was.

148

His next shot hit Anderson in the chest and drove him backward over the railing—which then cracked and toppled after him.

That left the three men in front of the porch, and Clint with four rounds.

He fired three more times. None of the three men ever had a chance to get their guns out. In rapid succession, they all fell on their backs, dead.

"Ho-lee crap!"

Clint turned and looked at Tara. Charlotte was getting to her feet.

"Are you all right?" he asked her.

"Y-yes," she said. "I—I felt the breeze from the bullet."

"Did you see that?" Tara asked Charlotte. "Did you *see* that?"

Clint ejected his spent shells, and in seconds his gun was loaded again. He wondered if Anderson had any other men in the area?

Tara was still staring at him, wide-eyed.

"You remember what I said inside?" she asked.

"What?"

"You might even be better with that gun than you are with your tallywacker."

Charlotte glared at him.

Chapter Thirty-Five

"Do we need to send for the sheriff?" Charlotte asked.

"Not just yet," Clint said.

"Why not?"

"Because Anderson knew the guns in the museum are fake," Clint said. "Who could've told him that?"

"You, me, Jayne, Walter," she replied, "or the sheriff."

"Right," Clint said, "and I'm hoping to find out it was the sheriff."

He looked at Tara.

"Can we still go and see your brother?"

"Sure thing," she said, "if you'll clean up a little here, first."

"There's a gulley over there," he said, pointing. They had passed it on the way. "Will that do?"

"Perfect!"

Clint dragged the five bodies over there, dumped them in, and tossed their guns in different directions.

"You got a buggy?" Tara asked.

"We do," Clint said, "and a driver."

"Then let's go."

They walked back to the buggy, where Frank greeted them happily.

"Am I glad to see you," he said. "I heard shots."

"I had to get rid of some varmints," Clint said. "Oh, this is Tara. She'll be coming with us."

"Sure thing," Frank said. "Where are we goin'?"

"This time, Tara will direct you," Charlotte said.

"Whatever you say, Miss."

Frank helped Charlotte in the buggy, and then held his hand out to Tara. She stroked his face before taking it.

"You're cute," she said.

Clint got in with them while an embarrassed Frank climbed onto his seat.

"Head back the way you came," Tara told him.

Once they were underway, Tara looked at Clint.

"Like I told you, you'll have to be careful of my brothers," she said. "You better let me go and talk to them first. The way you let Charlie talk to me."

"Will you be safe?"

She laughed.

"They're my brothers," she said, "but if you're worried, let me take Charlie with me."

"Why?"

"When we were in school my brother Witt had a crush on her," Tara said. "He'll be happy to see her."

Clint looked at Charlotte.

"It'll be all right," she assured him. "I'll go with her."

"Once we make sure they'll talk, and not kill," Tara said, "I'll come and get you."

"Okay," Clint said, thinking he would just follow them, the way he had Charlotte.

Once they got on the main road, Tara gave Frank directions. Within a few miles, they turned off onto a side road, again. This one took them to the house where Tara's brothers lived, with their aunt.

"The house you grew up in," Charlotte said.

"Yes," Tara said.

"You hated that house."

"I did," Tara said, "but I'm not going back for good." She looked around. "Stop here!"

Frank reined the horse in.

"If they see this buggy approachin' they might just shoot at it," she said. "I don't want cute Frank, there, getting' his head shot off." She looked at Clint. "Or you."

Clint stepped down, helped both women, and watched them walk off.

"You gonna follow 'em?" Frank asked.

"It worked before," Clint said.

"Can I come?" the driver asked. "Waitin' is hard."

"Do you have a gun?"

"No."

"Can you shoot?'

"I know one end of the gun from the other."

"Not good enough," Clint said. "You'll have to stay here. Besides, somebody has to watch the horse."

"Damn!" Frank swore.

Clint slapped him on the shoulder.

"We'll be back," he said, and started off after the two women.

Chapter Thirty-Six

He was able to follow both of their footprints and, before long, once again started to smell the beach. When he saw a large house up ahead, he stopped. This one was better cared for than the other, and had two stories. He was looking at the side of it, though, and if Tara and Charlotte were approaching the front, that was why he couldn't see them. There was some vegetation around it, enough to hide him as he started to work his way to the front.

***

"Are we going to have to talk to your aunt before we can talk to your brothers?" Charlotte asked.

"Probably. Why?"

"If I remember correctly from when we were young, she doesn't like me very much."

"That's because you could've got Witt to do anythin' you wanted," Tara pointed out. "Probably Lenny, too."

"Lenny?"

"Oh yeah," Tara said, as they approached the front of the house. "My older brother had a crush on you, too."

"I never knew that."

"He didn't want you to," Tara said. "And don't tell him you know now."

"I won't."

They mounted the porch together, and then Tara knocked on the door.

Tara's brother Lenny didn't answer the door. Neither did her brother Witt.

"Barney," she said.

"Hey, little sister," the middle brother, Barney, greeted. "Is that Charlie with you?"

"It sure is, Barney," Tara said. "Is Lenny around?"

"Somewhere," Barney said, with a shrug. "I think Aunt Emma's got him doin' some kind of chores."

"Where is she?"

"In her chair, as usual," Barney said. "You comin' in?"

"I'm comin' in," Tara said, with a nod.

"With her?"

"Yup."

"I mean, I don't mind," Barney said, "but you know Aunt Emma."

"Don't worry," Tara said, "I'll talk to her."

"Okay, then," Barney said, and backed away.

Barney was the odd man out in many ways. He was a beanpole, tall and skinny, while both Lenny and Witt were shorter and huskier. He was also much easier going than his brothers.

Tara and Charlotte entered the house and Barney closed the door.

"You know where Aunt Emma's chair is."

Tara did know, and even Charlotte knew, figuring it was the same chair from her childhood.

Tara led the way into the sitting room, where an old grey-haired woman sat in a high-backed wicker chair.

"Tara?" she said, in a tremulous voice. "Is that you? You come home?"

"Not to stay, Aunt Emma," Tara said.

"And who's that with you?"

Both Tara and Charlotte knew that the tremor in the voice was put on, and the woman's eyesight was as sharp as ever.

"It's Charlie, Aunt Emma," Tara said.

"What's that gal doin' here?"

"She wants to talk to Lenny. In fact, she's got a friend with her who wants to talk to Lenny."

"About what?"

"Those Blackbeard guns he found on the beach," Tara said.

"The guns that museum stole from us?" The woman had a walking stick in her left hand, and she banged it on the floor.

"That's right, Aunt Emma," Charlotte said. "And I'm sorry about that. I had nothing to do with it."

"You work for that man, don't ya?"

"I do."

"Then you ain't so innocent," the old woman said. "Who's this friend you brung wit'ya?"

"His name is Clint Adams."

Aunt Emma banged the walking stick again.

"Ain't that the varmint that's called the Gunsmith?" she asked.

"That's him," Tara said. "He's tryin' to find the real Blackbeard's real guns."

"Ain't they in the museum?"

"They say they been stole," Tara said.

"Actually," Charlotte chimed in, "they've been replaced with phonies."

The old woman squinted at Charlotte.

"You thinkin' my boys did that?"

"Mr. Adams just wants to ask if they know who might've done it," Charlotte said.

Aunt Emma did some thinking, then banged on the floor, again.

"You bring that feller in here and let me talk to him, first," she said.

"Yes, Aunt Emma," Tara said.

"I'll go get him," Charlotte said, because she didn't want Tara to do it and leave her alone with the old woman.

Chapter Thirty-Seven

Clint saw Charlotte come out of the house and rushed back up the dirt walk. He stepped out so she could see him.

"I knew you'd follow us," she said. "Aunt Emma wants to see you."

"Aunt Emma?"

"She's the head of the family, and she wants to talk to you before you talk to any of her nephews."

"Okay, lead the way."

He followed her back to the porch and through the front door. As Clint entered the sitting room he saw a woman with skin like parchment, sitting in a wicker chair holding a walking stick in her hand. The look on her face was stern, to say the least.

"Are you that Gunsmith?" she demanded.

"I am," he said. "Thank you for seeing me—"

"You two get out!" she snapped at the girls. "I'll talk to him alone."

"Aunt Emma—" Tara started, but the old woman cut her off.

"Out!" she snapped, banging the stick. "Wait out on the porch."

"Yes, Ma'am," Tara said. She and Charlotte left the room.

"You wanna set?" Aunt Emma asked Clint.

"Thank you—"

"Oh, stop bein' so damned polite and just set yerself down on that sofa."

"Yes, Ma'am."

"What's that feller's name that runs that museum?" she asked.

"Walter Fairchild?"

"He's a polecat!"

"I'm not going to disagree with you."

"Then why you workin' for him?" she asked. "Everythin' I heard about you, I ain't never heard that you was a polecat."

"I just want to find those guns and make sure they're real, and safe."

"You know my family's related to Blackbeard, don'tcha?" she asked.

"I've heard that."

"My boys found those guns and took them to the museum like they was supposed ta."

"I respect them for that."

The woman cackled.

"Ain't never heard nobody say they respected my boys," she said. "Hated, yes, and scared of, sure. Not respected. I'm gonna ask ya one more question."

"Okay."

"Do you think my boys stole them guns?"

"No, I don't."

"Why not?"

"No offense, Ma'am," Clint said, "but from everything I've heard about your nephews, I just don't think they'd be smart enough."

She cackled again, with delight, banging the floor with her stick.

"You know somethin'?" she asked. "You're all right."

"I've always thought so," he said, in place of a thank you.

"You go out and get them gals back in here from the porch, and I'll get my boys in here."

"Yes, Ma'am."

Clint got up and went out to the porch, where both Tara and Charlotte gave him a concerned look.

"She thinks I'm all right," Clint said.

"I knew she would," Tara said.

"So what now?" Charlotte asked. "Is she going to let you talk to Lenny?"

From inside they heard her yell, strong and loud, "Boys, you get your asses down here!"

Chapter Thirty-Eight

Clint and the girls went back inside. In the sitting room with Aunt Emma were three men, two short and husky. And Barney, the tall one who answered the door.

"My nephews," Aunt Emma said, "Lenny, Barney and Witt. Boys, this here's Clint Adams, the Gunsmith."

"Jesus," Witt said, "the real Gunsmith?"

"It's him," Tara said.

"What's he doin' here?" Lenny asked. He looked to be in his 30s, while his brothers were still in their 20s.

"He has some questions," Aunt Emma said. "You're gonna answer them."

"Why?" Lenny asked.

"Because I say so!" Aunt Emma snapped.

The three nephews stiffened, then gave their attention to Clint.

"Apparently," Clint said, "the flintlock and blunderbuss you found and . . . sold to the museum have been removed and replaced with phonies. Do you have any idea who could've done it?"

"Are you askin' if we done it?" Lenny asked.

"He's not," Aunt Emma. "He knows you boys wouldn't be smart enough to do somethin' like that."

"Hey—" Witt started.

"Aunt Emma—" Lenny began.

"Quiet!" Aunt Emma said. "He's right. You three ain't the brainiest boys I know."

Barney and Witt almost pouted, while Lenny glared at his aunt.

"Answer his questions," she said.

Barney looked at Clint.

"I don't know anybody who done that," he said.

"Neither do I," Witt said.

Clint looked at the older brother.

"I ain't as dumb as you think," he said to Clint, then looked at his aunt, "or as you think." He looked at Clint again. "To replace them guns, duplicates had to be made."

"That's true."

"There's only one person in Ocracoke who could do that," he said.

"And you know who he is," Clint said.

"Yeah."

"Will you take me to him?"

Lenny Teach looked at his Aunt Emma, then said to Clint, "Yeah."

***

The Teach family had enough horses, so they decided to let the buggy go back to the museum.

"Are you sure, Mr. Adams?" Frank asked.

"I'm sure, Frank. We'll meet you there."

"Yes, sir."

Clint waked back to the house, found the whole family out front with horses saddled, except for Aunt Emma.

"This one's for you," Lenny said, handing him the reins of a steeldust.

"Thanks."

They all mounted up.

"Where are we headed?" Clint asked.

"Ocracoke," Lenny said. "But we're gonna take a shortcut. For that we'll have to ride on the beach, a ways."

"We're with you," Clint told him.

They all mounted up and headed out, the three Teach boys in front, Clint, Tara and Charlotte bringing up the rear. Clint was happy to keep the brothers in front of him. They may not have been smart enough to pull this off, but they might just be dumb enough to try something.

Chapter Thirty-Nine

"I love this," Tara said, as they were riding on the beach. "The sand, the water, the sun . . . I sometimes ride here just to be alone with my thoughts."

"It is pretty," Clint agreed.

"I used to do it," Charlotte said, "before I started working for Walter Fairchild. Now I never have the time."

Up ahead they saw that the brothers were deep in conversation.

"Tara, who do Barney and Witt fear more, Lenny or your aunt?"

"It used to be Aunt Emma that we were all afraid of," she admitted, "but as Lenny gets older, he gets meaner."

"Are they going to pull something?" Clint asked her.

"Like what?" Charlotte asked.

"I don't know," Clint said. "Just something that Lenny tells them to do, not their aunt."

"Like taking the real guns from you if you find them?" Tara asked.

"Yes, like that."

"I honestly don't know," she said. "I know Lenny was really mad when he realized Charlie's boss cheated him."

"So if he sees a chance to get them back . . ." Clint said.

". . . he'll probably take it," Tara finished.

"I'll keep that in mind."

Eventually, Lenny led them off the beach and onto a little traveled road that seemed to be no more than a path. They had to ride single file for a while, and Clint made sure he took up the rear.

Eventually they moved onto the main road and he saw the town ahead of them. They rode in, drawing attention for several reasons. Clint had a feeling the Teach boys didn't usually ride in together like this, plus they had two women with them.

Lenny reined in and turned.

"You boys better head for a saloon, have yerselves a drink and wait for me," he told his brothers. "You wimmin can do whatever wimmin do when you're in town. Shop?"

"You stupid—" Tara started, but he wasn't listening.

"Adams, you better come along with me."

Lenny headed off, and Clint nodded to Charlotte that she should wait, and trotted after him.

Lenny took Clint down a side street and, for a moment, he thought the older Teach brother might be leading him into a trap, but then he saw where they were going when a Gunsmith Shop appeared up ahead.

Lenny reined in his horse in front of the store, and Clint followed.

"This is Tim Terry-Tom's shop."

"Tim Terry-Tom?" Clint asked.

"Hey," Lenny said, "that's his name, but everybody just calls him—"

"—Tim?"

Lenny looked at him like he was crazy and said, "No, Tom."

They dismounted and approached the door.

"So you're saying this Tom made those phonies?" Clint asked.

"No," Lenny said, "you asked me who might've had somethin' to do with it. Tom's the one I thought of."

"Okay," Clint said, "then after you introduce me, let me do the talking."

"Aunt Emma said I gotta do what you want, so okay."

"And if I ask you to step out," Clint went on, "just do it."

"Whatever you want," Lenny groused.

They entered the store, which seemed to be teeming with product, on the walls, and on shelves. The man standing behind the counter looked to be about 60.

"Tom?" Lenny said. "This here's Clint Adams. You know who he is?"

"Well, sure I do," Tom said. "He's the Gunsmith." He stuck out his hand. "Sure is a pleasure to have you in my shop." They shook hands. "What kin I do for ya?"

"I'm in town doing a job for the museum," Clint told him.

"I heard about that," Tom said. "That feller Fairchild, he's got you workin' on them Blackbeard guns, right?"

"That's right," Clint said. "How did you hear about that? From Lenny?"

"Not me," Lenny said.

Tom looked at Lenny, then at Clint, who got the message.

"Lenny," Clint said, "why don't you wait for me outside."

"I'll go and wait with my brothers in the saloon," Lenny said, and left.

After Lenny closed the door Tom looked both excited and agitated.

"How did Mr. Fairchild like them guns?" he asked Clint.

"Well, the real guns—" Clint started, not quite sure what Tom was talking about.

"No, no," Tom said, looking around as if there were others in the shop. He lowered his voice. "The phony ones."

"*You* made the phony ones?"

"Sure I did," Tom said. "Since you work for him, I thought you knew."

Quickly, Clint said, "I knew about the phony guns, but I didn't know you made them. That was fine work."

Tom looked pleased.

"Comin' from you, that's a compliment," Tom said, flattered. "Thank you, sir. But could you remind Mr. Fairchild that he ain't paid me yet?"

"I'm sure he'll get to it, Tom," Clint said, "don't worry."

Clint turned to leave.

"But wait!" Tom said. "Wasn't you in here lookin' for somethin'?"

"That's okay," Clint said. "I've got what I need." He started out the door, then said, "Lenny didn't tell me what saloon he and his brothers would be in."

Tom smiled.

"Aw, don't worry about that," he said, confidently, "I can guess."

***

When he stepped outside Clint decided to find Charlotte and Tara before going to look for Lenny and his brothers in the bar. With what he had just found out from Tom the gunsmith, he had an idea rolling around inside his head. But he needed to bounce it off of both Charlotte and Tara, first.

Chapter Forty

After finding Tara and Charlotte at a nearby dress shop—they actually did go shopping—and talking the idea over with them, Clint went looking for the Teach boys. Tara had mentioned the name of a saloon.

"They usually spend most of their time in town there," Tara said. "My husband used to do the same thing."

"Was he friends with your brothers?" Clint asked.

"He was," Tara said, "until they killed him."

Clint decided that was a story for another time.

***

He found Lenny, Barney and Witt Teach at a saloon called the Rusty Hinge. The batwings creaked mightily as he entered, and he wondered if that had anything to do with the name?

The three brothers were standing at the bar with beers. There were only two other men in the place, seated at separate tables. One appeared to be sleeping, and while the other one had his eyes open, he didn't seem to be seeing anything. They both had bottles of whiskey on the table in front of them.

"There he is," Lenny said to his brothers. "You find out anythin' from Tom?"

"I did," Clint said. "Can I get a beer?"

"Sure." Lenny waved to the bartender, who not only brought Clint a beer, but fresh ones for everybody.

"These are on me," Clint told him, and the man nodded.

Clint sipped his, found it icy cold. He wondered if the Rusty Hinge did a better business later in the day?

"Lenny, you'd like to get those guns back from the museum, right?"

"You bet your ass," Lenny said.

"What would you do with them?"

"Sell 'em to somebody honest," he said. "Onliest problem with that is, we don't know nobody honest."

"I think I can help you with that," Clint said. "I know some honest gun dealers who would love to have the flintlock and the blunderbuss."

"I thought it was a blunder-puss?" Barney said.

"It's buss," Lenny said. "Shut up." He turned his attention to Clint. "Whatayou got on your mind?"

Clint had checked with Tara first, to see if she thought her brothers would go along. She said she thought if it got them the guns back, they would.

Chapter Forty-One

After Clint left the Rusty Hinge he met Charlotte and Tara at a nearby café.

"How did it go?" Tara asked.

"They agreed."

"So what's next?" Charlotte asked.

"The sheriff."

"Why?" Tara asked.

"Because I can't just leave those bodies outside your house," he told her.

"They're in that gulley."

"Which is right outside your house," Clint said. "No, we've got to get them taken into town. That means telling the sheriff what happened. Then it'll be his job to bring them all in to the undertaker."

"And then what?" Charlotte asked.

"I want to see if I can figure out who they were working for."

"Who do you think they were working for?" Charlotte asked.

"Obviously somebody who's interested in those guns," Clint said.

"That bitch Jayne!" Charlotte snapped.

"Could be," Clint said.

"I hope it is," she said. "I want her to get hers."

Clint hadn't told Charlotte what he found out from Tim Terry-Tom, the gunsmith. He still didn't know how close she was to Walter Fairchild.

"Charlie, why don't you stay here in town while Tara and I go back to her house with the sheriff? No point in getting you involved."

"How will you tell Sheriff Lundigan how you got out there?" she asked. "And why you killed those men?"

"I'll think of something," he said. "Besides, Anderson and a couple of his men tried me in the telegraph office, and I'm pretty sure the clerk saw them leaving. I can convince the sheriff it was self-defense."

"I can tell him that," she offered.

"No, let Tara do that," Clint said. "Like I said, let's keep you—and the museum—out of it for now."

Reluctantly, she finally agreed. They left the café, and Clint took Tara with him to the sheriff's office.

***

"Mr. Adams!"

Lundigan had been lounging with his feet up on his desk. He hopped to his feet when they walked in.

"Hello, Tara."

She ignored him. He looked at Clint.

"I'm, uh, afraid I haven't found out anythin' about those guns, yet."

"That's okay," Clint said. "I'm here about something else."

"What's that?"

"You know a fella named Pete Anderson?"

"Yeah," Lundigan said, "him and a couple of his friends, they hire out for odd jobs."

"Well, they did their last one," Clint said.

"You mean . . . ?"

"They're dead, along with two more."

"Where?"

"Out at Tara's house."

He looked at Tara, she looked away.

"What happened?"

"They made a try at me," Clint said. "Five against one."

"And?"

"And it wasn't enough."

Lundigan's eyes went wide.

"You gunned them all?"

"He did it easy," Tara said, speaking for the first time. "Pop-pop-pop-pop-pop."

Lundigan swallowed.

"Where are they?"

"In a gulley near her house," Clint said, "just to get them out of the way."

"And what do you want me to do?"

"Your job," Clint said. "Go get them and take them to the undertaker."

"What else?"

"I want to go through their pockets."

"What for?"

"To see who they were working for."

"You think somebody sent them after you?"

"I know they did," Clint said. "What I don't know is who or why?"

"I can go through their pockets, see if there's anything there—"

"—and I'd have to trust you to tell me—and I don't."

Lundigan looked disappointed.

"All right," he said. "I'll send some men out to pick up those bodies tomorrow."

"Now," Clint said. "I want to go with them and check the pockets as the bodies are tossed onto a buckboard."

"You can do that when they get to town," Lundigan said. "At the under—"

"I'd have to trust that what's in their pockets now will still be there when they get here," Clint said, staring straight into the lawman's eyes. "I don't."

Chapter Forty-Two

Clint and Tara rode out and watched as four men collected the bodies from the gulley and tossed them onto a buckboard. Then they all went and had a cigarette while Clint went through the dead men's pockets.

"Anything?" Tara asked.

"Nothing," Clint said. "I've got one more . . ." He put his hand in Anderson's pocket and felt something. "Wait." He took it out.

"What is it?"

He came out with a piece of paper. It was an odd color, maybe lavender, and had a time and date written on it. The date was several days before.

"Does this mean anything to you?" he asked, handing it to her.

She accepted it, looked at it and handed it back.

"No," she said. "It looks like a time and day to meet somebody, but other than that . . ."

He refolded it and put it in his shirt pocket.

"There's something about it," he said, "but I can't— maybe it'll come to me, later."

"Is that all?" one of the men asked.

"Yeah," Clint said, "go ahead and take them to town."

As the buckboard pulled away, Clint and Tara mounted up.

"Where you headed now?" she asked.

"Back to the museum, I think," Clint said. "You might as well go back home."

"All I'll do is sit there and wonder what was goin' on," she said. "Can't I come with you?"

"Sure," he said, after a moment. "Why not?"

***

They rode to the museum and left their horses out front. Once inside Tara's eyes got wide and she kept swiveling her head to look around.

"You've never been here before?" he asked.

"No," she said, "never. It's so . . . big."

As they approached Jayne Kennedy's office he noticed the security man, Coates, standing in front of the door. At the same time, he heard someone call out to him from behind.

"Clint!"

He turned and saw Charlotte hurrying toward him.

"I just got here," she said. "What did you find out?"

"Not much," he admitted. "All I found on the dead men was a note in Anderson's pocket. Looks like a time and day for a meeting."

178

"Not a place?" she asked.

"No," he said. "I suppose he was meeting with his employer in the same place, each time."

"Can I see it?"

He took the note out of his pocket and passed it to her.

"Oh," she said, holding it in her hand but not unfolding it.

"What is it?"

"I can tell you something about it without even reading it," she said.

"What?"

"This paper," she said, "it's the same color as the note paper on Jayne Kennedy's desk."

"That's what rang a bell with me and I couldn't think of it," he said. "I saw her lavender paper, the color of her eyes, on her desk."

"Her eyes?" Charlotte said, and Tara rolled hers.

"He noticed her eyes," Tara said.

Clint took the note back.

"Never mind that," he said. "You know what this means?"

"That Anderson and his men were probably working for Jayne," Charlotte said.

"But why?" Tara asked. "Doesn't she work for the museum?"

"And Walter Fairchild," Clint said. "He could be part of this, too—or else she's trying to break away from him."

"That's more than likely," Charlotte said. "That bitch has always had her own agenda."

Clint wondered, briefly, why Charlotte sounded much more educated when she spoke than Tara did, if they went to school together. With the job she had, she must have gone on to college, something Tara and her brothers couldn't afford. But how did Charlotte afford it?

"Are you going to see her now" Charlotte asked.

"Yes."

"I'll just tag along."

"Why don't you," Clint said, and led the way to the door.

Chapter Forty-Three

Coates said, "Sir," As Clint approached.

"Coates," Clint said. "Good idea to post yourself out here."

"Actually, that was Miss Kennedy's idea," Coates said. "She's a smart lady."

Clint studied Coates, wondering if he had spent any time on top of Jayne Kennedy's desk?

"Is Miss Kennedy in?" he asked.

"Yes, sir." Coates knocked on the door and opened it. "Mr. Adams, Ma'am."

"Send him in," she said.

When he walked in with both Charlotte and Tara, Jayne looked surprised.

"I guess I should explain Mr. Coates' job to him a little better," she said. "He didn't tell me you had guests with you."

"Do you know Tara?" Clint asked.

"I don't," Jayne said, remaining behind her desk. To her left was a stack of her lavender note paper.

"It was her brothers who brought the Blackbeard piece to the museum."

"Ah," Jayne said, "Lenny's sister."

"You know my brother?" Tara had assumed that Lenny sold the pieces to Walter Fairchild.

"Let's just say we've met," she said. Again, Clint had to look at her desk top and wonder.

Clint looked over at the glass display case, with the guns inside. He walked closer and looked down. From that vantage point, they could have been real. At least one of them could have been Blackbeard's Gun.

"Have you found the real ones?" Jayne asked him.

He turned and looked at her.

"Yes."

She hesitated just a split second, then smiled and said, "That's wonderful! Where are they?"

"They'll be here tonight," Clint said. "They're being delivered."

"Tonight?"

He nodded.

"After you close here."

"Uh, shall I keep our security men on duty?"

"Just the night men," Clint said. "I'll be here to accept them."

"That's wonderful. Have you told Walter?"

"No," Clint said, "I thought maybe you could write him a note, and Charlotte could bring it to him."

"Sure," Charlotte said, picking up on what Clint wanted. "I'd be happy to."

"And what is Miss Teach, here, going to be doing?" Jayne asked.

"She's never been here before," Clint said. "I thought maybe we'd show her around. After all, she helped me get the guns back."

He could see Jayne's mind working.

"I see," Jayne said, finally. "Well . . . I suppose I could send Walter a note."

She sat down at her desk, grabbed a piece of her lavender note paper, and started to write.

"Make it short," Clint said. "Just tell him to come here tonight."

She looked up at Clint.

"Charlotte could just tell him that," she pointed out.

"You're in charge here," he told her. "A note from you would be best."

"Yes, all right." She went back to writing, finished. "There."

She stood and started to hold the note out to Charlotte, but Clint stepped up and grabbed it, surprising her. He then took the note from his pocket and compared them. The handwriting was the same.

"What are you doing?" she asked. "What's that?"

"It's the note you were foolish enough to write to your man, Pete Anderson," Clint said. "I took it from his pocket, after I killed him."

She sat down in her chair and stared at him.

"You killed somebody?"

"Anderson, and four of his friends."

She looked as if this news excited her.

"You killed five men?" she asked.

He didn't respond.

"So does this mean Charlotte's not going to deliver it to Walter?" Jayne asked.

She was very calm.

"Walter already knows," Clint said. "He'll be here tonight, too."

"Let me get this straight," Jayne said. "You think I had something to do with the guns being switched?"

"I do."

"Then if you think I have them, how are you getting them here tonight?"

"I didn't say you have them," Clint said. "I think you had something to do with them being switched."

"Ah," Jayne said. "So I don't have them."

"No," Clint said, "I do."

Chapter Forty-Four

But he didn't have them.

Jayne knew he didn't have them. He knew that. He was pretty sure she didn't have them but knew who did.

But how sure was she that he didn't have them?

She was going to have to check with the person who did.

"I'm going to show Tara around," Clint said. "I'll be back later, before the real pieces get here."

"Yeah, okay."

He smiled at her.

"I'll keep Coates on the door," he added. "We wouldn't want those phony ones to disappear, too."

Clint and Tara left the office. Charlotte was waiting outside.

"What now?" she asked.

"We go and tell Walter the same story," he said. "One of them is going to have to go and find out if they still have the pieces."

"How do we follow both of them?" Charlotte asked.

"We don't," Clint said.

"My brothers WILL," Tara said, "and they'll never see them."

"Tara, go and tell your brothers to get ready."

"Right,"

She ran off.

"And what do we do?"

"We go and talk to Walter, and then wait," Clint said.

"I hope this works," Charlotte said.

"Charlie, you and me both."

***

They went to Walter Fairchild's house and told him what they told Jayne.

"Tonight?" he asked. "Are you serious?"

"Dead serious," Clint said. "We'll have them back tonight."

"But that's great!"

They were in Fairchild's library. When they got there, they found him smoking a cigar and drinking brandy.

"It's good," Clint said, "but not great."

"Why not?"

"Because I still have to examine them," Clint said. "The original pieces could still be bogus."

"Jesus, don't say that!"

"Why?" Clint asked. "What's the difference. You didn't pay that much for them."

"I didn't cheat anybody, Clint," Fairchild said. "I don't like that word, 'cheat.'"

"Okay," Clint said, "you didn't cheat anybody. Look, I'm going to take Charlotte home. She wants to clean up and change. We'll see you at the museum later."

They left the house, and Clint spotted two of the Teach brothers waiting to follow Fairchild wherever he went. He had Barney and Witt, while Lenny had chosen to follow Jayne. His only worry was that Jayne said she knew Lenny. But Tara assured him that her brothers had nothing to do with the switch. He had to put his faith in the girl, who seemed to be different than the rest of her family.

"Where to now?" Charlotte asked.

"We have to go someplace and wait to hear from the Teach boys."

"My place?"

"I don't think so," he said. Sorry, Charlie, but they wouldn't find us there."

"Where then?"

"Tara's house."

"Why did I even ask."

"Charlie—"

"Never mind," she said. "I'm coming with you."

He smiled at her.

"I wouldn't have it any other way."

Chapter Forty-Five

Tara let them in and said, "I made coffee."

He noticed the two girls were glaring at each other.

"Let's have some," he said, "and you two can tell me how long you've been friends."

***

They were still in Tara's house when Barney came busting in the front door.

"Barney, what the hell?" Tara said.

"Sorry," Barney said, breathless. "Sorry, Lenny sent me."

"Lenny is supposed to be following Jayne, while you and Witt followed Fairchild."

"We all did," Barney said. "That is, we was gonna, but Fairchild never left his house."

"And?" Clint asked.

"Lenny followed that Kennedy woman to Fairchild's house."

"Are they still there?"

Barney nodded.

"Lenny sent me to get you."

"Well, let's go!"

***

Clint, Tara, Charlotte and Barney dismounted outside of Fairchild's house, where Lenny and Witt were waiting.

"Are they still inside?" Clint asked.

"They are," Lenny said.

"Any staff?"

"We saw a man and a woman leave together," Lenny said. "I think his cook might still be in there."

"And Jayne Kennedy?"

"Still in there."

"Okay," Clint said. "The rest of you wait out here. I'm going inside and get Blackbeard's guns."

"You sure you don't want at least one of us to go with ya?" Lenny asked.

"I'm sure," Clint said. "I think I can handle this myself."

He walked to the house, to the front door, tried it, found it open, and entered. He stopped just inside the door to listen, heard voices coming from the diningroom. He moved closer so he could hear.

". . . what he was talking about," Jayne Kennedy was saying.

"Well, I knew he didn't have the guns," Fairchild said. "You should have known that, too."

"He sounded so cocky," Jayne said.

"You shouldn't have come here, Jayne," Fairchild said. "You should have stuck to the plan."

"And what was the plan, Walter?" Clint asked, entering the room.

Instead of answering, Fairchild looked at Jayne.

"He followed you."

"So you lied?" Jayne said to Clint.

"Only because I wanted to fit in," Clint said. "After all, you've both been lying to me since I got here. Come on, Walter. If your plan was to steal the real guns and display some fakes, why even send for me?"

"That was the board's idea," Fairchild said, "and I can't veto every idea they come up with. Besides, I didn't really think of you as an expert."

"What did you think of me as?"

"Well," Fairchild said, "Now, no offense, but I just thought you were . . . you know, made up. I figured when you got here you'd be, uh, a dumb cowboy."

"Sorry to disappoint you," Clint said.

"I never thought you were dumb," Jayne told him.

"That's probably why you sent Anderson and his partners after me," Clint said. "To scare me off?"

She shrugged.

"Or kill me?"

She shrugged again.

He looked at the table, where Blackbeard's flintlock and blunderbuss lay on a cloth.

"Well," he said, "they look real." Clint glanced at them. "But you're still not sure, are you?"

"No," Fairchild said. "And now that I know you, I believe you can authenticate them."

"Well, I may not be a dumb cowboy, but I'm also not an acknowledged expert. So I've got one coming."

"Good," Fairchild said, "then we can get this all finished."

"No," Clint said, "*we* can't. I can. And the board. You two are out."

"What at you talking about?" Jayne asked.

"You two stole the real guns," Clint said. "The board's not going to like that."

"We didn't *steal* them," Fairchild said.

"Oh, I know," Clint said, "like you didn't cheat the Teach brothers."

"They are *not* descendants of Edward Teach!" Fairchild snapped.

"What does it matter? They did find the guns. And they should have been paid fairly."

"If you tell the board what I did, they'll thank me," Fairchild said.

"I doubt it," Clint said. "I think when I tell them you're both going to be fired."

J.R. Roberts

"I don't think so," Jayne Kennedy said, pointing a small, .25 Colt at him.

"Good girl!" Fairchild said. "Where'd you get that?"

"You don't think I wear suits like this because they're comfortable. I always have it on me," Jayne said. "Just in case."

"Just in case of what?" Fairchild asked.

She turned the gun toward him and fired. Fairchild grabbed his belly and slumped to the floor.

"So that was your plan all along?" Clint asked. "Kill him and steal the guns?"

"You don't think I've been sleeping with him because I liked it."

"I had a feeling about that."

"He couldn't handle me the way you did," she said. "Come on, Clint, you and me. I have a buyer who'll pay big for those guns."

"And if I say no?"

"Then I'll have to shoot you and leave with those guns," she said. "My buyer is waiting."

"There's people waiting outside for me," Clint said. "The Teach boys. They want their guns back."

She frowned.

"I'll go out the back."

"They've got the back covered. They may not have heard that first shot, but they'll probably hear a second."

He watched as the door to the kitchen slowly opened.

"I'll have to take that chance," she said. "I think I can handle Lenny. He and I have been, um, together a time or two."

"Made it easier to cheat him, didn't it?" Clint asked. "Sleeping with him?"

"He's dumb," she said, "like most men."

"I'll bet your problem isn't with men, Jayne," Clint said, "but with women."

"You mean Charlotte?" She laughed. "Oh, not little Charlotte."

"No," Clint said, "not Charlotte."

He watched as the cook reared back and then hit Jayne in the back of the head with a frying pan.

Chapter Forty-Six

Clint rolled over in bed and ran his forefinger down Tara's spine. When he got to the cleft between her buttocks she shivered.

"You really have to leave?" she asked.

"I do."

"Why not stay a few more days?"

"To tell you the truth, I've had enough of everyone here—except you."

She rolled over on her back and stretched, pulling her little tits taut for him.

"Have you had enough of me this morning?"

He put his hand on her belly, slid it down between her legs, where he found her already wet. He stroked her with one finger, then slid inside of her.

"Not nearly," he said.

She smiled.

"That's what I was hoping you'd say."

He rolled over on top of her while she opened her legs wide for him, and took his cock deep inside . . .

***

While Clint got dressed she said. "My brothers are pretty happy with you, you know."

"Tara, I told them, they're going to get paid if the guns are real."

"Oh, they say they're real," Tara assured him.

"Well, my expert is going to decide that this morning."

"Don't worry," she said. "They're real."

He went to the bed, kissed her, and said, "We'll see."

***

As Clint entered what was once Jayne Kennedy's office, Charlotte looked at him from the desk.

"So the board voted?" he asked.

She smiled.

"I'm the new curator."

"Congratulations."

"I'm sorry I couldn't see you last night," she said, "but I had a lot to do."

"Board meeting?" he asked.

She nodded.

"What did they decide."

"They're going to prosecute both Jayne and Walter," she said. "She's in jail, and he will be when he gets out of the hospital."

"Good," he said, "then it's all working out."

"They really thought you were just a dumb made-up legend?" she asked.

"I guess so," he said, with a sigh.

At that moment Coates came into the room.

"Got a fella out here says his name is Sandstone."

"That's my expert," Clint said.

"Send him in," Charlotte said.

Coates went out, and then a grey bearded man, about 5 foot 5, came in, wearing a black suit and wire-framed eyeglasses.

"Clint."

"Sandy," Clint said, and they shook hands. "This is Charlotte Goodrich, the museum curator. Charlotte, Professor Henry Sandstone."

"Happy to meet you," Sandstone said. "And the guns?"

"Right there," Clint said, indicating the glass display case.

Charlotte walked over, unlocked the case, and then stood back.

Sandstone walked to the case, slid it open, and reached in for the flintlock. He examined it, set it down, picked up the blunderbuss, then also set it down.

He looked at Clint and Charlotte with tears in his eyes and said, "Oh my."

Coming September 27, 2018

THE GUNSMITH
440
Lost Man

For more information
visit: www.speakingvolumes.us

On Sale Now!

THE GUNSMITH
438

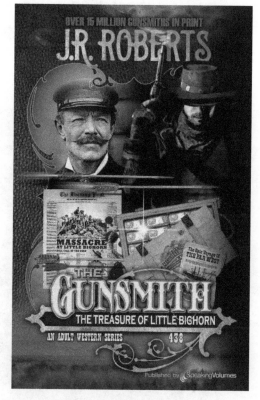

For more information
visit:

On Sale Now!

THE GUNSMITH
437

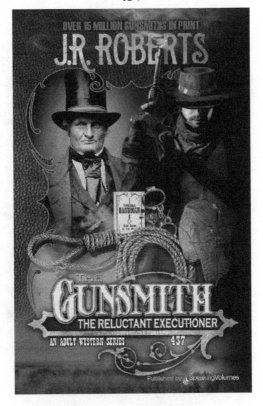

For more information
visit:

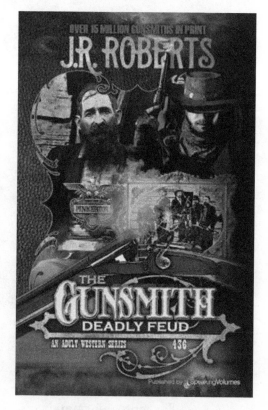

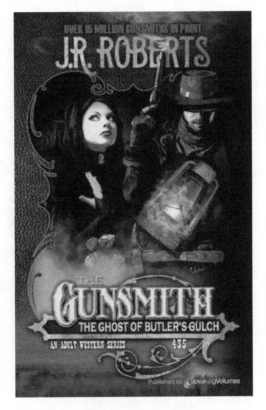

On Sale Now!

THE GUNSMITH
434

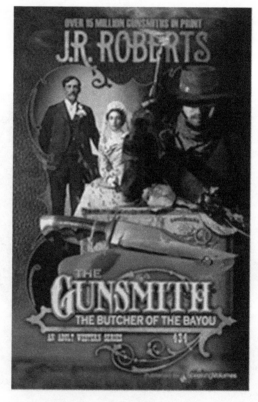

For more information
visit:

On Sale Now!

THE GUNSMITH
433

For more information
visit: www.speakingvolumes.us

On Sale Now!

THE GUNSMITH
432

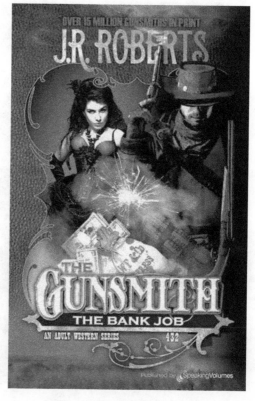

**For more information
visit:** www.speakingvolumes.us

On Sale Now!

THE GUNSMITH
431

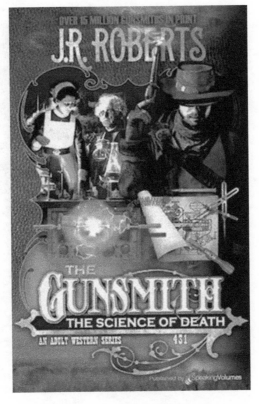

For more information
visit:

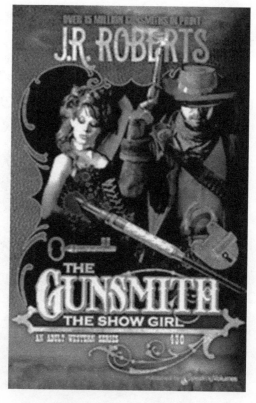

On Sale Now!

Lady Gunsmith 5
The Portrait of Gavin Doyle

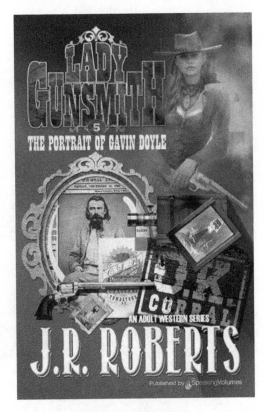

For more information
visit: www.speakingvolumes.us

On Sale Now!

Lady Gunsmith
A New Adult Western Series
Books 1-4

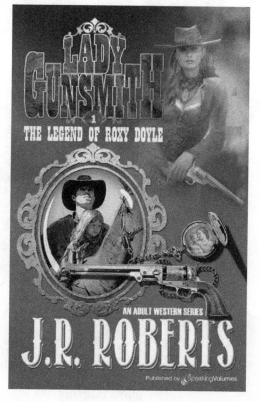

**For more information
visit:** www.speakingvolumes.us

On Sale Now!

ANGEL EYES *series*
by
Award-Winning Author
Robert J. Randisi (J.R. Roberts)

For more information
visit: www.speakingvolumes.us

On Sale Now!

TRACKER *series*
by
Award-Winning Author
Robert J. Randisi (J.R. Roberts)

On Sale Now!

MOUNTAIN JACK PIKE *series*
by
Award-Winning Author
Robert J. Randisi (J.R. Roberts)

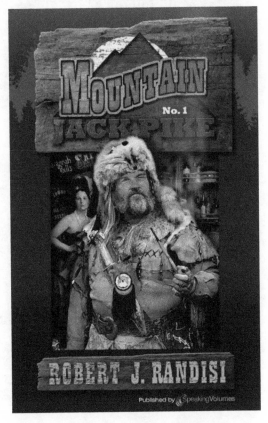

For more information
visit: www.speakingvolumes.us

Sign up for free and bargain books

Join the Speaking Volumes mailing list

Text

ILOVEBOOKS

to 22828 **to get started.**